Jaco Jacobs is the most popular and prolific children's author in Afrikaans. He has published more than 140 books and sold over a million copies. Jaco is also a well-known columnist, blogger, freelance journalist and translator. He lives in Bloemfontein, South Africa.

Kobus Geldenhuys is an award-winning translator who received the South African Academy for Arts and Science prize for Translated Children's and Youth Literature in Afrikaans for his translation of the third book in Cressida Cowell's popular children's series *How To Train Your Dragon* in Afrikaans.

Jim Tierney is an acclaimed book designer and illustrator. In 2011, he was awarded a New Visual Artist award and in in 2016, he won a Regional Design Award for Amy Stewart's *Girl Waits With Gun*. He lives in Brooklyn with his wife Sara Wood.

A GOOD DAY FOR CLIMBING TREES

JACO JACOBS

Illustrated by Jim Tierney

Translated from Afrikaans by Kobus Geldenhuys

ROCK THE BOAT

J
JAC

A Rock the Boat Book
First published by Rock the Boat, an imprint of Oneworld Publications, 2018
Originally published in Afrikaans in 2015 as *'n Goeie dag vir boomklim*

Copyright © Jaco Jacobs, 2015, 2018
English translation copyright © Kobus Geldenhuys, 2018

ISBN 978-1-78607-317-4
eISBN 978-1-78607-318-1

This book has been published with the support of
Arts Council England and BookTrust

Supported using public funding by
**ARTS COUNCIL
ENGLAND**

Typeset by Fakenham Prepress Solutions, Fakenham, Norfolk, NR21 8NN
Printed and bound in Great Britain by Clays Ltd, St Ives plc

Oneworld Publications
10 Bloomsbury Street
London WC1B 3SR

Stay up to date with the latest books,
special offers, and exclusive content from
Rock the Boat with our monthly newsletter

Sign up on our website
www.rocktheboat.london

MIX
Paper from
responsible sources
FSC® C018072

9/18   B+T $11.99

For Elize, Mia and Emma –
who keep me from
becoming invisible

Doing the Dishes

'Hey, you deaf doofus, didn't you hear the doorbell?'

I clenched my teeth and squirted a green blob of Sunlight liquid into the kitchen sink.

When someone shouts at you like that, there are a few things you can do.

Option one: you can pretend to be deaf and ignore it. Which isn't a good idea if your older brother is the one shouting at you. In any case, not if you have an older brother like Donovan.

Option two: you can threaten to break the shouter's nose if he calls you a doofus again. But in this case that would be plain stupid. Donovan had provincial colours in swimming, lifted weights every day and drank those protein shakes that give you humongous muscles. To top it all, at the age of fifteen he had perfected the art of the wedgie. All the underpants in my cupboard were stretched out.

Option three: you can point out to him, in a very friendly manner, that the person who rang the bell definitely isn't looking for you, seeing that your best (and only) friend has gone to America with his parents for the December holidays. But, once again, you stand a good chance of getting a wedgie for your trouble.

Option four: you can make use of the normal pecking order and tell your little brother to open the door. But in our case the normal pecking order no longer existed. Adrian was only nine years old but he'd bought himself a position above mine. Long story short: I was currently my little brother's personal slave. If I wanted any pocket money during the holidays, I'd better make sure I didn't rub him up the wrong way.

Option five: you can leave the dishes, dry your hands and go and open the door.

Guess which option I chose.

The girl on our porch looked a little older than me. She was wearing faded blue jeans and her brown hair was tied in a ponytail. Her braces flashed in the sunshine as she smiled nervously.

'Hello? Erm...I'm looking for Donovan? Adrian...erm...invited me?' She spoke in question marks.

I sighed and called over my shoulder, 'Donovan, you have another client!'

The girl shuffled her feet awkwardly and her face turned bright red.

If my mum and dad were ever to find out what was happening in this house in broad daylight, they would need serious therapy. Fortunately they both worked during the day and were blissfully unaware of the fact that their youngest son was renting out their eldest son to schoolgirls. There's a word for that. And it's illegal.

Adrian said I was being dumb – it was just an innocent self-esteem workshop.

He was the kind of nine-year-old who knew words like 'self-esteem'. My dad said he would be either a millionaire by the time he turned eighteen, or serving his first prison sentence. My little brother was the richest nine-year-old I knew. He started his money making schemes in nursery school – during the rugby season he got his little friends to bet on the weekend games. By the time a furious mother found out about it, he had made quite a bit of money already. Adrian was also the only child I knew who had been expelled from nursery school. Not even the fact that my mum was a lawyer could save him. Since going to primary school, he had been making most of his money by supplying the tuck shop with cheap sweets. At least, we suspected that that was how he made most of his money.

Adrian was constantly hatching all kinds of mysterious plans to make money. Dad said he preferred not to know all the details. His latest plan (Adrian's plan, not Dad's) was to rent out Donovan for kissing lessons.

Yep, girls like the one with the braces who was standing on our porch, blushing like mad, paid for the privilege to kiss my older brother.

The year before, Donovan had started gelling his hair and lifting weights and had transformed into a girl magnet. At swimming training in the afternoons, a whole crowd of schoolgirls hung around the pool to see him in his Speedos. He had broken more girls' hearts than Chad le Clos had swimming records. But it seemed the girls hadn't wised up because at least three or four had come for kissing lessons since the beginning of the holidays. They would disappear with Donovan into the shaded *lapa* next to our pool for half an hour. When they reappeared, their hair was messed up, their lipstick smudged and they were smiling like mad. I had no idea how much Adrian charged for the kissing lessons and what percentage Donovan got. Maybe Donovan played along for the fun of it, because he seemed to have girls on the brain. And pool chlorine. No wonder he had scraped through Grade Nine by the skin of his Speedos.

The girl on the porch cleared her throat and rubbed her jeans self-consciously. She looked like she wanted to run away.

If Donovan spent as much time behind his schoolbooks as he spent in front of the mirror with his hair gel and comb, I bet he would've scored at least three As. He was taking his time but I didn't invite the girl inside. My mum wasn't a lawyer for nothing – I knew what 'accomplice' meant. I wanted no part whatsoever in those so-called 'self-esteem workshops' that Adrian and Donovan were running.

Finally, Donovan showed up. His hair was gelled perfectly and he reeked of the expensive aftershave Mum had bought Dad for his birthday.

'Hi.' He greeted the girl with a broad smile and shoved me aside like a doorstop he didn't want to trip over. 'Let's go and sit outside in the *lapa*.'

The girl giggled nervously and turned a deeper shade of scarlet before they disappeared down the veranda.

With a sigh, I closed the front door and walked back to the kitchen.

Outside in the garden the pool pump was going *chug-chug-chug*.

The fridge was humming like a purring cat.

At the front gate Mr Bones was barking at the reverend's wife, who was walking past with her German shepherd.

A few minutes later, Adrian walked into the kitchen.

'Are you done with the dishes yet, Marnus?' he asked in a bossy voice while getting some orange juice from the fridge.

The three of us were supposed to take turns to tidy up the kitchen. But at the start of the holidays I had begged for an advance on my pocket money and bought myself a second-hand PlayStation Portable from Adrian. He, in turn, had bought it from one of his friends. The stupid thing broke a week later but Adrian refused to give my money back, because he said I'd bought it without a guarantee or warranty. I wasn't even sure what those words meant. The bottom line was: I had to do the dishes every day and clean the kitchen in exchange for pocket money from my nine-year-old brother.

My life sucked.

I was officially having the worst December holidays ever. I wished we could go for our usual holiday by the sea but my mum and dad had decided that we'd go to a game reserve for three weeks during the June holidays, so they didn't want to take a lot of leave during December. Besides, my mum was working on a Very Important Court Case and my dad was hoping that this year's Christmas spending would save his sports shop from going under, which meant that him taking leave now was out of the question.

The doorbell played 'Jingle Bells' again. The week before, my dad had replaced our doorbell with one that played Christmas tunes. This was his pathetic attempt at bringing a little Christmas cheer into our house. I suspected that by June the following year, when we were scheduled to go to the game reserve, the doorbell would still be playing 'Jingle Bells', because by Easter this year no one had got around to taking the Christmas tree down.

'Aren't you going to answer the door?' asked Adrian.

He was spilling some orange juice on the table. The table I had just cleaned.

My dental bill was going to be sky-high after the holidays, because I was grinding my teeth down to stumps.

I dried my hands on the dishcloth again and walked to the front door.

Where, of course, another girl was waiting.

This one was blonde and looked about my age. But her eyes were the first thing you noticed about her – large and bright blue, with dark lashes.

'Sorry, Donovan is still busy,' I mumbled. 'You'll have to wait your turn.'

A frown appeared between her eyes. 'What turn? And who's Donovan?'

'Aren't you here for the kissing lessons?' I asked.

To the left of the frown, one eyebrow went up a centimetre or two, and she smiled a semi-smile. 'Kissing lessons?'

My face started to glow. 'Erm...forget about it. Sorry. Can I help you?'

'Will you sign my petition?' she asked and held a piece of paper out to me.

Surprised, I stared at the page. It looked like it had been torn out of a notebook. On it was a list of signatures, addresses and telephone numbers.

'Erm...I don't think so,' I said. My mum always said you should never put your signature on paper before you understand every single word that's written on it. Obviously Adrian learned words like 'guarantee' and 'warranty' from her.

'It's for a good cause,' said the girl.

'What cause?' I asked.

Her semi-smile became a full smile. 'If you want, I can go and show you.' She pointed at the dishcloth in my hand. 'Or would you rather dry the dishes?'

9

My face heated up another couple of degrees. 'Erm...I don't know...'

I was still stammering an excuse when she started giggling softly. Her face tilted forward as she tried to cover her laughter with her hand but I could see the teasing glint in her eyes.

'Come on. I'm sure the dishes can wait a few minutes. When I've shown you what the petition is about, you'll definitely sign it.'

She took my hand and pulled me in the direction of the front gate.

'By the way, my name is Leila.'

2

The Tree At The Centre
Of The Universe

'A tree?'

I looked at Leila in surprise.

She nodded. 'A white karee. Scientific name: *Rhus pendulina*.'

'Pleased to meet you, tree,' I said.

The tree stood silent and slightly sad in the early-morning heat.

I ran my hand over its rough trunk. 'Is this an endangered species or something?'

'Not really,' said Leila without taking her eyes off the tree. She looked up as if she wanted to make sure that every leaf was still in its place. 'Many people plant white karees in their gardens. They don't need that much water and they grow fast.' She sounded a little like a TV presenter.

I frowned. 'So why did you draw up the petition to save this tree?'

Leila looked at me for a long time, as if she was trying to decide what she thought of me.

I wondered what she saw.

I didn't have blond hair, blue eyes, bulging muscles and a tan like my eldest brother. I didn't have a snub nose covered in freckles and an adorably cute face like my little brother. Not that I thought my little brother's face was adorably cute but old ladies seemed to think so – seconds before Adrian convinced them to part with their money by some sly trick.

My hair was brown and slightly too long and full of cowlicks that made it stand out in all directions. My eyes were green. When I was with my brothers, I was always the last one anyone noticed. Marnus-in-the-middle. Sometimes it felt like I was invisible.

Slowly Leila let out a deep breath while still staring at me intently. 'This isn't just another tree,' she said. 'This is The Tree At The Centre Of The Universe.' You could hear the capital letters in her voice.

Before I could stop myself, I burst out laughing. This girl was off her rocker. What had possessed me to walk all the way to this small park, three blocks from home, so that she could show me a tree?

'The Tree At The Centre Of The Universe?' I asked.

'Forget it.' Her eyes flashed. 'I thought...
Never mind. Just drop it.'

She sounded furious, and I expected her to
twirl around and walk away. But from the way
she was glaring at me it was obvious that I was
the one who had to buzz off.

I didn't need an invitation. With a shrug, I
turned to go home. I didn't feel like making small
talk with a half-crazy girl. Besides, I had to finish
the dishes.

There were still twenty-three days left of the
horrible summer holidays.

Yep, I counted them.

And the sooner I could get today's dishes
done, the better. Then there would only be
another twenty-two sinks filled with dirty dishes.

'When I was small, I always came to play in
this park,' said the girl behind me. Her voice was
so soft that I almost didn't hear what she said.

I stopped.

'I learned to climb trees in this one.'

I turned around but it seemed like she
didn't even know that I was standing there and
staring at her. It looked as if she was talking to
the tree.

'Not all trees are good for climbing. A white
karee has rough bark. You can easily lose your
skin when you slip, so it isn't really ideal for

climbing. But this one's branches are low and thick, and they grow close to each other, which means you can almost get to the very top. It's perfect for tree-climbing.' She was caressing the trunk of the tree.

Then we heard a noise, turned around and saw a white pickup approaching across the lawn.

'That's them,' said Leila in a dark voice.

I didn't know who 'them' were. Maybe those guys in the white jackets who were fetching her to lock her up in a place for people who talked to trees?

I felt guilty about that thought.

The pickup stopped and two men got out. One of them had a clipboard with some papers that made him look very important. His shirt was stretched tightly across his tummy, as if the buttons would pop at any moment, and his forehead was shiny with sweat. The other man was tall and thin, with a sharp face and a narrow little moustache. He didn't even glance in our direction – he immediately began to study the tree.

'I drew up a petition,' Leila said to the man with the clipboard. She held the paper with the signatures out to him as if she wanted to show that her papers were as important as his. 'Almost fifty people have signed it already.'

From the tone of her voice you could hear that Leila was counting the signatures on her petition like I was counting the remaining dishwashing days.

I suddenly felt bad for not wanting to put my signature on the paper.

'Too late,' said the man without looking up from his clipboard. 'Paperwork's done.'

'But this is a petition!' said Leila. Her blue eyes flashed. 'People signed it because they don't want the tree to be chopped down. Almost *fifty* people. People who *care*. You can't just carry on.' Her voice was seesawing up and down.

The man shrugged. 'Try the municipal manager.'

'The municipal manager?' Leila asked hopefully.

'On holiday,' said the man. 'Only coming back end of January.'

It seemed like it was too much trouble for him to speak in full sentences.

The thin man started circling the tree with precise steps. He looked at it in the same way Donovan and Adrian and I looked at the last bit of Sunday-lunch pudding left in the bowl. It was as if he wasn't planning to only cut down the tree – he wanted to eat it as well.

'When are you planning to cut it down?' Leila's voice sounded like it was racing over a speed bump.

'Laying the pipe in early January,' answered the man. 'Tree must fall today.'

Leila drew in her breath sharply. Her eyes went wide. She stripped off her sandals and kicked them aside. Before I could ask what she was doing, she swung round and started nipping up the tree.

'Where are you going?' asked the man, surprised.

Leila's summery skirt was flapping around her legs. I stood there with the two men from the municipality and watched as she scampered up and made herself comfortable on a branch. Only her two bare feet could be seen dangling from the leaves. The soles of her feet were dirty and brown, like the inside of her sandals.

The red-faced man from the municipality gave me an imploring look, as if he expected me to do something.

I just shrugged.

The man sighed and produced a handkerchief from somewhere. Slowly, he wiped the sweat off his red forehead. 'That girl.' He shook his head. 'Talk to her. The pipeline. No choice. Tree's in the way.'

'The tree was here first!' shouted Leila.

'Don't worry, Mr Venter, as soon as I have my team here, one of them can climb up with a ladder and get the girl down from there,' said the thin man with the rat face. His tone of voice was threatening.

'No one touches me,' came Leila's voice from above us.

I looked up into the tree. Strips of light flashed blindingly among the leaves, almost like when the sun plays on water. An unexpected dizziness made the light swim in front of my eyes. It looked as if the tree was slowly turning round and round. For a moment, I shut my eyes tightly.

I thought of my eldest brother, who was going to spend the entire day lying beside the pool *again* and threaten to give me wedgies if I didn't wait on him with cold drinks.

I thought of my little brother, the snotty-nosed slave driver who ordered me to make his bed every morning and tidy his room in exchange for pocket money.

I thought of the doorbell playing 'Jingle Bells' and the girl with the braces who'd paid to have my brother kiss her.

I thought of my school report. In the final exams I'd scored seventy-seven percent for maths – more than ten percent better than the previous term – and I was top of my class in Afrikaans.

Mr Fourie said it was because I wrote such good compositions. But my dad hadn't even noticed my report because he was too busy giving Donovan an earful about his rotten marks and praising Adrian for his brilliant report. No matter what happened, I always disappeared somewhere between my two brothers. Always somewhere in the middle, where no one ever saw me.

When I opened my eyes, I looked down and noticed the red and white dishcloth over my shoulder. I had completely forgotten about it – I had actually walked all the way here, three blocks from home, with a dishcloth over my shoulder. It felt like the kind of strange thing Leila might do. Maybe her strangeness was contagious.

I thought of the piles of dishes waiting for me at home.

Above my head, Leila's two dirty feet were dangling to and fro among the green leaves.

Somewhere a turtle dove was cooing.

The red-faced man from the municipality was blowing his nose.

I think you sometimes do things in the blink of an eye, without thinking – things that change your life.

You ask someone to marry you in the middle of a horror movie, like my dad asked my mum.

You decide at five in the morning that you feel like ice cream, like my dad's sister, Aunt Karla, did last year, and then you're paralysed in a car accident at the crack of dawn.

Or you follow a weird girl into a tree with a dishcloth over your shoulder.

3

A Lady in Pink

'You can't stay up there all day. You'll have to come down sometime.'

I couldn't help feeling a little sorry for the red-faced man from the municipality. He had unbuttoned the top two buttons of his shirt and, by this time, his handkerchief was full of sweaty stains. It looked as if he was wishing he was lying by a pool with an ice-cold drink in his hand rather than having to talk to two children sitting in a tree.

I didn't know how long we'd been sitting up there but it felt like at least an hour or two.

'He's right,' I whispered to Leila. 'We'll have to get down sooner or later.'

Leila smiled at me. The tree was throwing dappled green shadows on her face. 'You're braver than I thought,' she said.

I didn't feel brave at all. I was thirsty and my bum was hurting from sitting on the hard branch. On top of that, I was sure I would need to go to the loo pretty soon. And I couldn't get rid of the feeling that we were in trouble.

In the meantime, two more municipal pickups had arrived. On the back of one of the pickups were men with chainsaws and other equipment. They were sitting around, bored and waiting for us to get down from the tree.

'I still say we should just get them down from there,' growled Rat-face.

'We can't use violence,' said Red-face. 'They're two kids. Can you imagine what the press would say?'

Leila and I grinned at each other. Didn't they realize that we could hear every word?

Like Leila, I lightly kicked the air with my bare feet. I had taken off my sneakers and put them in a fork in the branches. I was hoping Leila couldn't smell my socks. At least it was nice and cool up in the tree. It smelt like the small shed on my grandfather's farm, where he kept the firewood for winter. Somewhere above us a bird was chirping among the branches.

I smiled when I suddenly thought of something my dad sometimes said. When he was feeling down in the dumps or when things went wrong, he would say, 'Yep, today's a good day for climbing trees.' Lately my dad was down in the dumps quite often.

Suddenly the calm was shattered by some ear-splitting yapping.

'Trixi, Georgie, pipe down, my darlings,' said a voice somewhere below us. A voice that sounded vaguely familiar. 'What's going on here?'

My stomach flip-flopped and I pushed some leaves out of the way to see who the voice belonged to.

'It's Mrs Merriman,' I whispered to Leila in alarm. 'She lives in the same street as us. If she sees me, she's going to call my mum and dad.'

My mum said Mrs Merriman was eccentric. I thought that was just a nice word for 'freaking weird'. She always wore pink clothes and even her grey hair had a touch of pink in it. She came to this park every day to walk her two poodles, George and Trixibelle. At least once a month she rang our doorbell to collect money for the SPCA, the Society for the Prevention of Cruelty to Animals. My mum always told us to ignore her but my dad always opened the door and patiently listened to her descriptions of the dire needs of the poor animals.

I heard Red-face explain about the tree that had to be felled to make place for the pipeline.

'What a pity,' said Mrs Merriman. 'Such a beautiful tree.'

'It's going to be even more of a pity if people don't have water to drink,' Red-face replied gruffly. 'Nor doggies like these. Can't do our job. Two kids sitting up there in the tree. Refuse to get down.'

'Strange,' said Mrs Merriman. She shaded her eyes with one hand and peered up.

I quickly let go of the leaves so that she couldn't see my face.

The rustling of the leaves made George and Trixibelle growl suspiciously.

I was starting to get worried. If *Mrs Merriman* thought this was strange, it wasn't a good sign. After all, she had pink hair.

A mobile phone rang.

'Hello?' answered Red-face.

Leila and I looked at each other.

'His ringtone is Justin Bieber?' Leila stifled her laughter with her hand.

I shrugged. Maybe Red-face had a teenage daughter at home. Donovan once uploaded a heavy-metal ringtone for my mum. I wish I could've seen the look on the faces of her stiff-lipped colleagues when they heard her phone ring for the first time.

'The office,' said Red-face to Rat-face after ending the call. 'We have to go back.'

Surprised, Leila and I watched the men get into the pickups.

'Don't think you've won!' Red-face shouted through his open window as he drove off. 'We'll be back!'

When they were gone, Leila and I gave each other a high five. Her hand was soft and cool against mine. She was grinning from ear to ear.

'So, what now?' I asked, stretching out my arm that was getting stiff by then. 'Shall we get down?'

'You heard what that man said,' said Leila. 'They'll be back.'

I said nothing. I'd guessed she was going to say that.

We jumped with fright when a voice suddenly spoke right below us. I grabbed hold of the branch to stop myself from falling off.

For a moment I'd forgotten all about Mrs Merriman.

'Could I perhaps bring you two darlings some cold drinks?' she called. 'You must be thirsty by now.'

4

The Bowling Club

For a long time Leila and I sat in the tree without talking to each other. The silence didn't seem to bother her. She sat with her head tilted to one side, as if she was listening intently to the chirping of the birds and the drone of distant traffic.

After a while, I cleared my throat. 'Erm...I need to get to a toilet sometime soon.'

My cheeks felt warm. Why did it feel so awkward to say the word 'toilet' in front of a girl? After all, girls also go to the toilet. Maybe it was because I didn't have a sister.

'Try the bowling club,' said Leila.

She pointed to the other side of the lawn, where some cars were parked. From where we sat, I could see elderly men and women in white clothes standing around on the bowling green, and from time to time the balls hit each other with a sharp *click-click* sound.

'My grandma always said, "The older you get, the weaker your bladder gets." I think most bowls players are old, so I bet you there are toilets there. But hurry – before the people from the municipality come back.'

I suddenly realized she expected me to stay up in the tree with her. Who said I didn't have better things to do? This should have made me angry but for some reason it made me feel rather...proud. It felt as if she trusted me.

Carefully, I climbed down. My legs were feeling a little wobbly when I finally stood on firm ground. How long had I been up in the tree for? My watch was lying on the kitchen table because I'd taken it off before I started doing the dishes. My mobile phone was in my room. If Donovan and Adrian dared read my texts, I was going to kill them.

'Aren't you coming down as well?' I asked Leila. 'There's no one here.'

'Rather not,' came her voice from above. 'I think it's better if one of us stays up here all the time. Just in case.'

In case of what? I preferred not to ask.

The sun was grilling the back of my neck as I walked in the direction of the bowling club. I tried not to think too hard about what Leila was doing. Maybe Red-face went to fetch the police to get us out of the tree. Maybe they were going to use tear gas or rubber bullets, like on

TV. Donovan and Adrian were going to be *so* jealous.

The gate to the bowling club was open. It was quiet, apart from the sound of balls *click-click*ing against each other every now and then, each time followed by polite applause. A sign above the fence said, *Private property. No entry. Trespassers will be prosecuted.*

I tried my best to look like I wasn't a trespasser. It was harder than it sounds. When you're thirteen years old, and wearing a Quiksilver T-shirt with a red and white dishcloth over your shoulder, it isn't easy to walk into a bowling club without being noticed by anyone. I couldn't believe that I didn't leave the dishcloth in the tree.

But, miracle of miracles, no one spotted me.

I had no trouble finding the signs with the little man and woman. I slipped into the men's toilet.

It was nice and cool inside, and it smelt good. Crisp white towels were draped over wall rails and a small bottle of soap had been placed on every washbasin. I quickly locked myself in a cubicle, in case someone walked in and discovered me.

When I was done, I washed my hands while looking at myself in the mirror above the basin. I was almost disappointed to see that I still looked exactly the same as when I got up that morning – mousy brown hair that was slightly too long and refused to lie flat, green eyes, slightly protruding ears. That wasn't really how I thought someone who was breaking the law should look. I was sure that it was illegal to sit in a tree to prevent the municipality from chopping it down. My mum would know for certain. And being in this men's room was definitely illegal. The sign at the gate said so.

'What are you doing here?'

The gruff voice made my tummy turn and my legs became jelly.

For some reason, the man filling the entire door frame made me think of a gigantic Lego man – he was sort of round and square at the same time. His shoulders were broad and his chest looked like a wine barrel under his khaki shirt. His head was shaved and shiny, and his brown face was full of large freckles that looked as if they had been painted on. Even the hands hanging by his sides looked like a Lego man's pincer hands.

'Erm...my grandpa plays bowls here?' I stammered. I immediately wished I could erase the question mark at the end of my sentence.

The man made a rumbling sound that came from deep inside his chest. 'Look, boy, I've been the caretaker at this club for years. I know every member's children and grandchildren. I even know the names of most of their dogs. So, why don't you rather own up?'

I swallowed. There was no way I could get away – Lego man filled the entire door.

'I...Well...It all began when I was doing the dishes this morning...' I started telling him. At least the dishcloth over my shoulder should have convinced him that this time I was telling the truth.

He remained expressionless while I told him about Leila and the tree and the men from the municipality.

'And then I needed a loo,' I concluded.

For a moment his facial expression remained frozen, like that of a plastic figurine. Then, unexpectedly, he laughed. 'I know exactly which tree you're talking about. Walk with me. I have to meet this Leila girl.'

5

On an Island

By the time the caretaker and I arrived at the tree, Mrs Merriman and her two poodles were sitting on a picnic blanket underneath.

Above their heads Leila's feet were still dangling from the leaves.

'Pleased to meet you, ma'am,' said the caretaker with a nod of his head. If he was surprised to see a lady with pink hair and two pink poodles sitting under the tree on a pink picnic blanket, he was too polite to show it. 'I'm John Carelse, caretaker of the bowling club.'

Mrs Merriman held out her hand. 'Theresa Merriman,' she said. 'And these are George and Trixibelle.'

'Erm...and this is Leila,' I said and pointed up in the tree.

Leila peeped out from behind the leaves and smiled at the caretaker. In one hand she held a cold drink can.

'Marnus, Mr Carelse, how about something to drink?' asked Mrs Merriman. 'I brought enough. They're nice and cold.'

'Please call me John,' the caretaker said to Mrs Merriman. 'Or Caretaker or Uncle John,' he said looking at me and Leila. 'That's what most people call me.' He took a can from Mrs Merriman. 'Thanks a lot.'

Mrs Merriman moved aside a bit and gestured for us to join her on the picnic blanket.

The caretaker plonked his big body down on the edge of the blanket.

I remained standing, feeling awkward.

'So, the two of you are going to try and save this tree?' the caretaker asked and cracked open his can.

'Actually, Leila came up with the plan,' I said.

'They can't chop down the tree while we're sitting in it,' Leila said.

The caretaker leaned back, propping himself up on his hands on the grass, and stared up into the tree. 'This is a good tree,' he said in a calm, peaceful voice. 'A tree like this should be for ever.'

Leila and I said nothing.

But Mrs Merriman leaned forward and placed her hand on top of one of the caretaker's hands. 'What beautiful words, John,' she said. 'A tree like this *should* be for ever.' It looked as if she'd sipped the words through her straw and was tasting them.

The caretaker sighed. 'There are many things that should be for ever. I grew up in Cape Town. District Six. Those were good times. District Six was the kind of place that had its very own sounds and smells and tastes. But in another way, those were bad times. In the seventies the government decided all the non-white people had to move away from the area. By that time I was already married and working in Johannesburg. But my younger brother was still living at home with my mum and the rest of the family. On the day the bulldozers came to demolish the houses, he and his friend lay down in front of them.'

I tried to imagine what it must feel like to lie on the ground while a huge bulldozer is thundering towards you.

'And did it work?' I asked.

'Of course not, silly!' Leila said impatiently. 'Haven't you ever heard of District Six?'

Uncle John smiled at me. 'No one could be bothered with my brother and his pal. The police chased them away with *sjamboks*, and the houses were flattened. But then again, we live in different times now. I'm glad that someone is still prepared to fight for a tree.' He looked at his watch. 'You'll have to excuse me. I must be off.

There's a big tournament today, and I don't get paid to lounge around in the park. Thanks a lot for the cold drink, Mrs Merriman.'

'Theresa, please,' she said.

The caretaker nodded. Then he looked at me, and up into the tree. 'I'll drop by again later,' he said.

When he was gone, the three of us were quiet for a while. I think Leila and Mrs Merriman were also thinking of the caretaker's story. It must have taken a huge amount of guts to lie down in front of a bulldozer. If Rat-face or Red-face returned in their municipal pickup and came at us with *sjamboks*, I'd be out of there like a shot, but I wouldn't tell Leila that.

My eyes wandered to Leila's branch.

I couldn't decide whether I was supposed to sit on the picnic blanket with Mrs Merriman, or climb back into the tree. Maybe Mrs Merriman saw that I was uncomfortable because she winked at me and pointed up into the tree.

Relieved, I scrambled back up.

Leila smiled when I sat down again next to her on the branch. 'I was wondering whether you'd come back.' The leaves were still casting green shadows on her face.

I shrugged. 'This is a good day for climbing trees,' I said.

Leila gave me a puzzled look but I didn't quite know what my dad's saying meant, so I didn't try to explain.

'I wonder how long it will take those people from the municipality to come back,' said Mrs Merriman.

Neither Leila nor I tried to guess. We just sat there and watched one of Mrs Merriman's doggies get up and lift its leg against the tree.

'Would you mind if I stayed here for a little longer?' asked Mrs Merriman. 'I promise not to be a nuisance.'

'Of course you can stay,' said Leila.

Mrs Merriman rummaged in her picnic bag and took out a pencil and a magazine. She paged through it until she got to a crossword puzzle then hummed softly while she completed it. Every so often, she stopped humming and pondered a clue for a moment before filling in the answer.

It was getting really hot. I started to miss our pool – even though I knew that Donovan was probably lying beside it, waiting for me to come and swim so that he could try and drown me or torture me with cozzie wedgies.

Talking about wedgies, it felt as if the branch we were sitting on was giving me one. I shifted around uncomfortably and sighed, utterly bored.

'You're stranded on an island,' said Leila, 'and you have only three things with you. An eraser, a feather duster and a roll of toilet paper. What would you do with them?'

I frowned. 'What?'

'What would you do with those three things?' she asked. 'It's a game we always played when we were on a long road trip and I was bored in the car.'

I shrugged. 'I don't know. There's probably nothing you can do with an eraser when you're stranded on an island.'

'Well, if the two of you aren't going to use that eraser, I wouldn't mind borrowing it,' said Mrs Merriman. 'I've just misspelled the name of a tennis player and I didn't bring along my eraser.'

'There's nothing you can do with any of those things if you're stranded on an island,' I muttered.

'That's what you think!' said Leila. Her eyes were sparkling and she bit her bottom lip. 'Maybe it's a brightly coloured eraser – then you can break it into pieces and throw them into the water to lure fish. Then you can catch and eat them!'

'I've never heard of fish that eat erasers,' I grumbled.

When Leila said nothing back, Mrs Merriman asked, 'And what about the feather duster?'

'Maybe there are cannibals on the island,' said Leila as she yawned and leaned back against the tree trunk. 'Which means I can use the duster as a fan to keep the cannibal king cool – and in return for that he won't gobble me up.'

'And the toilet paper?' I wanted to know.

Leila rolled her eyes. 'Duh! What d'you think you do with toilet paper?'

My face was aflame. That thing with girls and toilets again.

It looked as if Leila was struggling not to laugh out loud.

For a while, we sat in silence and stared at the park. From time to time, some joggers ran past, or people walking their dogs or pushing children in prams. Only a few people saw Leila and me perched up in the tree. Mrs Merriman and her poodles got a couple of strange looks but she must have been used to that because they didn't seem to bother her at all.

At lunchtime, Mrs Merriman produced a container filled with meat pies from her picnic basket and gave them to us. George and Trixibelle got one each as well. It really looked like she was planning to spend the entire day under the tree.

After eating, Leila climbed down. She stretched her legs a bit and chatted to Mrs Merriman. Then she walked in the direction of the bowling club. The caretaker had said we were welcome to use the restrooms any time.

When Leila disappeared through the gate, I considered climbing down. I could easily sneak off while she was away. All I had to do was tell Mrs Merriman that I still had to go and do the rest of the dishes.

But when I pushed the leaves aside, my heart sank.

'Someone's coming this way,' said Mrs Merriman.

'Someone called Trouble,' I sighed.

Donovan stopped under the tree. 'Good afternoon, ma'am,' he greeted Mrs Merriman.

George and Trixibelle growled at him not to come any closer.

'Good afternoon, young man,' greeted Mrs Merriman. 'How can I help you?' She sounded like a receptionist – '*Good afternoon, and welcome to Leila and Marnus's branch office.*'

Donovan raised the tip of his cap slightly and shifted his weight awkwardly. 'Erm...my brother has disappeared. We've been looking for him all day. One of my pals sent me a text saying that he saw him here in the park.' He looked up. Obviously he knew exactly where I was. 'Marnus, what the hell are you doing up there in the tree like a baboon?' He looked at Mrs Merriman apologetically. 'Excuse me, ma'am. Marnus, Mum found out that you disappeared and she almost called the police to report you missing. You'd better come home.'

'I'm staying right here,' I said. It's easier to play hardball when you're sitting high up in a tree.

Donovan glared at me. His protein-drink muscles were bulging under his tight, help-me-look-strong shirt. I could see he was itching to give me the worst wedgie in the history of mankind, one that would go into the record books. But then he just shrugged as if to say, *Don't say I didn't warn you.* He dug his mobile phone out of his trouser pocket.

I swallowed anxiously. I knew trouble was coming my way.

'Hello, Ma,' said Donovan. Pause. 'Yes, he's here. He's sitting in a tree.' Pause. 'No, there's a lady with him.' He lowered the phone and looked up. 'Marnus, Ma wants to speak to you.'

I swallowed again, feeling even more anxious. 'I can't come down,' I said. 'I promised Leila one of us would stay up here all the time.'

'He doesn't want to come down, Ma,' reported Donovan with a grin. 'He said something about a girl.'

I felt sorry for his ears, because even from up there in the tree I could hear my mum's voice buzzing like an outraged wasp. I knew that tone of voice well. It was the tone of voice that drove hardened criminals to tears when she grilled them in court.

Donovan lowered the phone again. 'Ma says you're to go home immediately, or else...' He gave Mrs Merriman another apologetic look. 'My mother is a lawyer and she can talk quite dirty when she's angry, ma'am. Marnus, Ma says if you don't go home straight away, she's going to – Hey, what're you doing? Gimme back my phone!'

He swung around, taken by surprise.

Leila was standing behind him, with his mobile in her hand. Confronting my brother, she looked even tinier than the first time I saw her. But Donovan didn't dare take his phone back from her.

Leila held the mobile to her ear. 'Hello, ma'am,' she said. 'My name is Leila. Marnus is sitting in the tree in the park. Everything's cool. This is just an act of protest. I think it's our constitutional right. Don't worry – we're quite safe.'

She gave the phone back to Donovan, swiftly climbed into the tree and joined me on the branch. As if nothing had happened. As if she hadn't just told my mum that 'everything's cool'. I wished I could have seen my mum's face.

Donovan listened to my mum for a moment. 'Sure, Ma,' he said and ended the call. He looked up at me. 'You're freaking crazy.' He gave Mrs Merriman yet another apologetic look. 'Excuse me, ma'am, but he is.'

He turned around and started walking back home.

6

A Circle of Candles

When dusk fell, Mrs Merriman put her crossword puzzles away. She got up and folded up the pink picnic blanket.

The two poodles yawned and stretched themselves.

'Listen, you two, unfortunately it's time for me to go home,' she said, 'but I don't want to leave you here alone.'

I looked at Mrs Merriman with new eyes after that day. She might have been old and pink but no one dared mess with her. That was a lesson my dad had learned earlier that afternoon.

In his heyday my dad had played for the Cheetahs rugby team. If he hadn't torn a ligament, he could have played for the Springboks. Well, that was what he always told us while we watched rugby and he downed a couple of beers. Strangely enough, not one of his three sons enjoyed watching rugby with him. He was always shouting at the players, as if he was angry with each of them personally. I think Dad was actually angry that his sports shop wasn't doing too well. Donovan was the only one of us who had inherited his rugby talent, even though I suspected he enjoyed swimming more. I also played rugby but for the third team. And Adrian refused to take part in sport because he said it interfered with his business dealings.

My mum was still working on her high-profile case, so she had sent my dad to fetch me that afternoon.

'Dammit, Marnus, you're not seven years old any more! What are you doing up there in the tree? Get down! Don't make me come and get you...'

I was angry and anxious at the same time – and, of course, mortally ashamed that Leila and Mrs Merriman were seeing and hearing everything.

And then Mrs Merriman started talking to him.

I wish I could remember everything she said to him. But it basically amounted to the fact that Leila and I were incredibly brave and that she admired us for what we were doing and that my dad should give us a break.

I couldn't believe it but she managed to convince him. Well, it did help that there was a Rugby Sevens series on and that one of the semi-finals was on television that afternoon.

As my dad walked away, he just muttered something about my mum, who wasn't going to be happy at all, and that he would have to bear the brunt.

'We'll be OK, Mrs Merriman.' Leila's voice pulled me back to the present. 'Don't worry.'

'I'll stay here with them,' said a soft, serene voice.

I looked down in surprise.

A woman had walked up to the tree unnoticed.

Mrs Merriman nodded. 'OK then. See you two tomorrow,' she said with a small wave at Leila and me.

The woman beneath the tree was standing quietly, watching Mrs Merriman and the dogs walk away. Her long blonde hair was blowing gently in the evening breeze that had sprung up.

I recognized her eyes immediately. She could only be Leila's mum – they had the same large, bright-blue eyes.

'Leila,' she said with a sigh.

Leila said nothing.

I waved at the lady.

'I'll fetch us some blankets,' she said. 'And something to eat.'

I remembered then that Leila had said the park was close to their home.

'Let's see who can spot the evening star first,' said Leila when her mum had left.

We sat in silence for a while.

'I win,' she said, pointing. 'There it is, at the tip of that branch.' She laughed. 'Never mind – I cheated. I know exactly where it appears every night.'

By that time my body was feeling as if I'd been wrestling with an elephant. One of my legs was numb; I'd been sitting on it for too long.

'We can't sleep up here in the tree,' I said. 'We'll fall and break our necks.'

'We can take turns,' she suggested.

'The people from the municipality didn't come back today,' I said. 'What are the chances they'll come back in the middle of the night to cut down a tree?'

I thought I heard the leaves rustle as Leila shrugged.

'I don't know but I'm still not going to take a chance,' she said. 'You can go home if you want. I'm staying right here.'

I clambered down. Once on the ground, I jumped around stiffly until I could feel both my legs again. Then I sat down with my back against the tree trunk.

A while later, Leila's mum approached in the dusk. She carried a pile of blankets and a basket.

'What's your name?' she asked while putting everything down under the tree.

'Marnus, ma'am,' I answered.

I hoped she knew that this whole tree business was her daughter's idea, not mine.

A plastic bag rustled and a moment later a match was struck. She lit a few candles and placed them in a circle around the tree.

Then she held a blanket out to me. I took it, feeling embarrassed.

It seemed Leila and her mother didn't speak to each other. And it seemed they were equally strange. The candles placed around the tree looked like something from a movie or a storybook. I must admit, in a way I quite liked it. Leila and her mother looked like people who were used to doing things by candlelight. In our house we only used candles during power outages, and that usually led to a mad search for the candles and matches.

I spread the blanket on the lawn and lay down on it.

The wind had gone quiet. Crickets were giving a concert in the dark; in the distance music played and dogs barked; and over in the street a car whizzed past occasionally.

One of the cars turned in at the park. I sat up and watched the lights slowly thread their way through the trees and come closer. The engine got louder and I had to hold my hand in front of my face to protect my eyes against the sharp light that suddenly fell on us. A door was flung open and someone approached.

'Marnus?'

Oh no. I should've expected this. I jumped up and quickly climbed back into the tree.

'Yes, Mum?' I asked from the safety of the bottom branch.

Moths and dust were whirling in the sharp car lights. It looked like my mum's work clothes had not creased one little bit since that morning, and every strand of her hair was still in place. She looked very different from Leila's mother, with her creased, multicoloured floral skirt and tousled, limp ponytail.

'Enough of this nonsense, Marnus. Come home. I'm going to strangle your father. I can't believe he left you here.'

Actually, that shouldn't have surprised her. One Saturday my dad took us three boys to a rugby game, and afterwards he forgot Adrian at the stadium. Though that wasn't entirely Dad's fault – Adrian had been taking orders and was queuing for people who didn't want to go and buy refreshments while the game was on. At a solid profit, of course. Donovan and I didn't say

anything because we wanted to see how long it would take my dad to realize Adrian wasn't in the car. We were parked in our garage when he finally noticed that there were only three of us in the car.

'Marnus, get down from there. I won't tell you again. This is your last warning.'

I took a deep breath. 'Mum, I'm going to sleep here tonight. Leila and I are going to stay in the tree until the people from the municipality decide not to chop it down.' I swallowed. 'You always say you have to fight for what's right. That's what Leila and I are doing.'

I thought again of the caretaker's story about the bulldozers, and for some reason I felt guilty.

'Don't be ridiculous, Marnus!' she barked. 'This isn't like that at all.'

'It *is*,' I argued. 'Only, we're not fighting in a court – we're fighting, erm, in a tree.'

Sometimes an idea makes a lot of sense while it's still in your head, but as soon as it slips out of your mouth, it sounds like you've been sniffing toilet spray.

Mum sighed. 'Please, Marnus, I don't have the strength for this. It's been a long and difficult day. I'll call the municipality tomorrow and find out if all the correct procedures have been followed in order to fell the tree. Maybe there's a loophole somewhere. There's nothing that you or I, or...' she looked at Leila's feet peeping out from the leaves like two small, pale, nocturnal animals, '...anyone else can do about this right now. Come on down and get into the car.'

'I'm not going home,' I said resolutely. 'No one at home ever notices me. I'm just everyone's slave. If Donovan hadn't split on me, you would only have found out that I was gone by tomorrow morning.'

'Rubbish!' said Mum. 'You don't have to climb into a bloody tree if you want attention.' Her voice was rising dangerously.

I suddenly felt like telling her how Donovan bullied me and how Adrian blackmailed me, but if Donovan found out that I'd squealed on him, I would have to spend the rest of my life up there in the tree. And I was dependent on Adrian for pocket money for the rest of the holidays.

I folded my arms. 'I'm staying right here.'

Checkmate.

Mum and I glared at each other.

Leila's mother cleared her throat. 'At least this is a safe neighbourhood,' she said cautiously. Her voice sounded soft in comparison to my mum's. 'I won't leave them alone tonight.'

Mum pinched the piece of skin between her eyebrows and closed her eyes. She always did that when she was trying to calm herself down. Then she shook her head and walked back to the car. I'd known her long enough to know that she hadn't given up on this battle at all. But she was losing her temper, and my mum believed that a lawyer always stayed cool and collected.

The Renault's engine sputtered angrily when she drove off.

When the noise of the car had faded, Leila said in the dark, 'You and your mum are actually very alike.'

7

Noises in the Night

I guessed I must have fallen asleep because I was woken by someone softly calling my name.

'Marnus!' An anxious whisper.

Confused, I sat up. For a moment I had no idea where I was. Then I remembered the tree.

'There's...something here,' Leila's mother whispered.

I heard her fiddling around in the dark and then *whoosh*, a match was struck. Her face looked ghostly in the yellow spot of light, and her eyes were large and panicky. She held the burning match above the picnic basket.

'Something – or someone – looted our picnic basket,' she said.

I folded my arms in front of my chest and looked around. The match died and immediately everything was pitch-dark again. I could hear my heart beating in my ears. It felt as if the darkness was watching us. Suddenly I wished I was home and in my bed.

Mr Fourie said my compositions showed that I had a rich imagination. Sometimes a good imagination wasn't such a good thing at all. In my mind's eye I could see newspaper headlines about two children and a woman who were murdered in a park late at night.

Leila's mother struck another match and struggled to relight one of the candles. At last the flame flickered faintly.

'Maybe you should come and sit up here,' Leila suggested.

My imagination was definitely not good enough to form a picture of Mum climbing into a tree but Leila's mother didn't need any encouragement. I could see who Leila inherited her tree-climbing talent from. Her mum gathered her skirt in a bundle around her legs and climbed up in a flash. For a moment I considered rather staying down on the ground. Wouldn't it be weird to spend the night in a tree with Leila as well as her mother?

But then I heard something in the dark. Close to me.

Leila and her mum yelled.

I'm sure I broke some tree-climbing record.

In silence we sat and listened. The wind was rustling through the leaves and it blew out the candle below us. I could hardly breathe.

In the pitch-dark, paper rustled, and then we heard some groaning and greedy eating sounds.

I crossed my fingers lest Leila and her mum started yelling like girls do at the movies. I was the only man up there in the tree, even though I was only thirteen years old and the smallest guy in my class. I guess I was supposed to try and keep them calm or protect them or something. But I didn't really know how you were supposed to keep girls and their mothers calm when sitting up in a tree while some night stalker was stealing your food. Had my mum been there, she would've chased that villain away by now. Mum was used to scaring murderers and robbers and other thugs out of their senses. Even Dad was scared of her, although he'd never admit it.

It felt like an eternity before the eating sounds stopped.

'Has he left?' Leila whispered.

No one answered.

'Hello?' I asked cautiously. I thought of the one-eyed man who was always begging at the traffic light in front of the university and gave me the shivers when he peeped into the car with that one eye of his.

Everything was dead quiet.

'He's definitely left,' said Leila.

'I'm staying right here,' said her mother.

When it became evident that the night stalker wasn't planning to come back immediately, I started to relax.

I yawned.

For the thousandth time I wished that I had my mobile phone with me so that I could see what the time was or at least play games to while away the hours. But the battery probably would have become flat already because I had the oldest phone in our house. I think Noah used a Nokia like mine on the Ark. I had no idea how long I'd dozed off for. Poor Leila probably hadn't slept a wink because it had been my turn to sleep first.

I had goosebumps again but fortunately this time it wasn't due to mysterious noises in the dark – the night air was quite cool.

The silence was getting on my nerves, so I cleared my throat.

'Erm...you're stranded on an island,' I said, 'and you have only three things with you. A newspaper...a piece of string and...a chocolate bar. What would you do with them?'

Leila laughed softly. 'The newspaper is easy – I'd fold it into a sun hat...and build some kind of sunshade so that I didn't burn red like a lobster.'

'If the string was long enough, I'd weave a hammock,' said Leila's mum. 'Then I could lie in the hammock and read the newspaper until someone showed up to rescue me.'

I smiled. 'The chocolate bar is the easiest. I would've eaten it.'

'No!' said Leila's mum. 'I would rather put it somewhere to attract bugs. I read that when you're stranded without food, insects are an excellent source of protein.'

'Gross!' said Leila. 'If it was a cannibal island, I'd give the chocolate to the cannibal prince. Maybe it would be love at first sight when he tasted it, and then I'd become a cannibal princess and stay on the island for the rest of my life.'

'Gross!' I said. 'You want to become a cannibal?'

'Yep, you guys better make sure you don't end up on my island,' Leila said in a dark voice. 'Anything's better than eating bugs – even a little human flesh. Grrr!'

We laughed.

But suddenly someone coughed right below the tree.

Our laughing turned into hysterical screaming. Fortunately, Leila and her mum screamed so loudly that you could barely hear me.

'Don't worry, it's only me!' said a voice.

'It's Uncle John,' I said shakily. 'The caretaker.'

A bright torch beam shone up into the tree and blinded me.

'Do you need company?' he asked.

'OK,' said Leila with a shaky laugh. 'What would you do with a chocolate bar if you were stranded on an island?'

Uncle John thought for a moment. 'That depends on who's stranded on the island with me. Who knows? Maybe I'd share it.'

8

No Comment

For the first time in my life I woke up under a tree.

The sun was shining in my face and I slowly opened my eyes.

'Morning, sleepyhead,' Leila greeted me from her branch above.

She sounded cheerful for someone who had spent almost all night sitting in a tree. Sometime during the early hours she had broken her own rule and the three of us had got down and fallen asleep on our blankets but clearly Leila was already back at her post.

Leila's mum yawned and stretched. There were leaves in her tousled hair.

There was no sign of the caretaker.

My clothes felt damp from the dew. I tried to flatten my hair with my hand. It felt as if one of Adrian's hamsters had slept in my mouth. If my mum or dad returned, I would muster up the nerve to ask for a toothbrush and toothpaste.

A little bird was chirping up in the tree. I did a double take when I saw the upside-down food basket. Now that it was daylight, I could see for the first time how much damage the mysterious night stalker had done. Breadcrumbs and torn crisp packets were scattered on the grass.

'Shame, maybe it was a hungry tramp,' Leila's mum said and started clearing up the mess.

'Look who's here,' said Leila.

The caretaker was approaching us from the direction of the bowling green. He was carrying a tray with mugs.

'I hope with all my heart there's coffee in those mugs,' said Leila's mum.

'Morning!' greeted Uncle John merrily. 'How are the tree protectors this morning? I brought coffee and breakfast bars.'

The smell of fresh coffee was enough to lure Leila down.

While drinking my coffee, I looked at the bowling green. Water sprinklers were *tsick-tsick-tsick*ing rhythmically and a water curtain was flashing in the sun.

'I switched the sprayers on early this morning,' said Uncle John.

'Isn't it boring to be the caretaker of a bowling green?' I asked. 'I think I'd rather be caretaker at a rugby stadium. Then I could meet famous rugby players and watch every match for free. I don't know of any famous bowls players.'

Uncle John laughed. 'You'd be surprised. Here at our club we have two Springbok players.' He leaned against the tree and stared, lost in thought, into the distance while blowing on his coffee to cool it down. 'Bowls is actually a fantastic game. It's a pity that people know so little about it.' There was a strange smile on his lips. 'Do you know why bowls players wear white clothes? I think they're practising to become angels, because that's what a group of bowls players reminds me of – angels playing around on green grass.' He sighed. 'My wife loved bowls. She played in the provincial team, until the cancer got the better of her. If you ask me, we'll be playing all day long in heaven...'

'Bowls?' I asked and pulled a face.

'No, I don't think only bowls,' said the caretaker with a grin. 'Whatever we want to play. We won't work or struggle or get sick – we'll just play and play and play, from morning till night.'

I pulled a face again. 'I don't think you'd be able to play rugby in heaven. My dad swears way too much when he watches a game.'

The caretaker's belly jiggled with laughter. He emptied his mug in a couple of gulps and shook the last few drops out on the grass. 'I have to

go,' he said. 'I'll fetch the tray and mugs later.'
He gestured with his head. 'Seems you have an
early-morning guest.'

A young guy was walking towards us. He
was tall and thin, with a beard. The beard
didn't really suit his young face – it looked like
a disguise, or as if a large, fluffy animal was
clinging to his jaw for dear life. He wore a pair
of bright-green pants that fitted tightly around
his ankles, and black and white sneakers. In his
hand he held a notebook.

'You think he's from the municipality?' asked
Leila's mum.

'I don't know,' said Leila. 'He doesn't really
look like someone who works for the municipality but we'd better get back into the tree.'

By the time the man was standing under the
tree, Leila and I were back on our branch.

'Good morning,' greeted the man in a deep
voice that seemed to come from the depths of
his beard. He was speaking to Leila's mum. 'My
name is Junior du Toit. I'm a journalist at the
Morning News.' He looked up into the tree.
When he saw Leila and me, he smiled. 'I'd like
to do a story about the two of you.'

Leila and I looked at each other in surprise.

'Where did the paper hear about us?' Leila
whispered to me.

I shrugged.

Junior du Toit opened his notebook. 'Someone called us. Someone who offered to sell the story exclusively to us.'

I groaned. 'Bet you that was my little brother,' I whispered apologetically to Leila. 'Adrian would do absolutely anything to try and make money.'

'Unfortunately we don't pay for stories,' the journalist explained. 'But I'd really like to speak to the two of you, if you don't mind?' He gave Leila's mum a respectful look. 'I assume you're the mother of one of them?'

The lady shrugged. 'Leila is my daughter,' she said.

The journalist looked up again. 'Did you sleep in the tree all night?'

Leila and I looked at each other.

'We took turns to sleep on the ground,' she said. 'My mum was with us the whole time.'

Junior wrote in his notebook. 'And are you protesting against them chopping down the tree?'

'The tree's been here for years,' said Leila. 'Why can't the municipality bury their pipe somewhere else? Uncle John – he's the caretaker at the bowling green – says a tree like this should be for ever. Put that in your article.'

'Look who's here again,' I said with a sigh.

The white municipal pickup was coming towards us through the trees.

Red-face and Rat-face got out. Though it was still early, Red-face already had sweaty patches under his arms.

'You two still here?' he asked with a sigh in his voice. 'Morning,' he greeted Leila's mum and the journalist. 'I hope you're here to speak to the kids. Talk some sense into their heads. This tree has to come down. No later than today. We're a day behind schedule.'

'We're staying right here!' Leila said cockily.

Red-face quickly turned into Purple-face. 'Where are your parents?' he asked. 'Alone all night in a park? What kind of mother and father would allow something like that?'

Leila's mum cleared her throat. 'I am her mother.'

Red-face seemed to calm down slightly. 'Ma'am,' he said, 'speak to your daughter. Please. Sorry about the tree. Really. But please understand. We have no choice.'

The journalist was watching us as if we were actors in a movie, and occasionally jotted something down in his notebook.

'Leila,' said her mum, like the previous evening.

Leila ignored her, like the previous evening.

Red-face wiped his forehead with a hanky and muttered something about children of today being out of control and parents of today not being able to keep their children in check.

Rat-face didn't say a word. He just scowled at us as if he wished he could cut down the tree with a chainsaw while we were still in it. To me he looked like the kind of man who would enjoy driving a bulldozer.

'Sir, I'm Junior du Toit, reporter at the *Morning News*,' the journalist said and held out his hand to Red-face. 'I assume you're from the municipality? Would you mind if I asked you some questions? Why must the tree be chopped down?'

It looked as if Red-face was choking on something. 'I...I don't speak to the press!' he mumbled. 'No comment. Call the municipal public relations officer. Not that it will be of any use. She's on leave.' He yanked open the door of the pickup and pointed a threatening finger at Leila and me. 'You two! You've taken this business too far. Way too far!'

9

Dumped

'A journalist came to see us,' Leila announced when Mrs Merriman showed up a while later with her two poodles.

Mrs Merriman stopped to examine a sandy, grassless patch. George and Trixibelle were sniffing around excitedly.

'A dog's been here,' said Mrs Merriman. 'A big one – look at its paw prints.'

Leila and I looked at each other. I could see we were thinking exactly the same thing: was our night-time visitor a dog?

Leila's mum had gone home to shower and put on some fresh clothes. I'd hoped that Leila would ask her mum to bring us a mobile phone or a watch or something. Even board games would be OK, although I really hated board games. Monopoly went on for ages and Adrian always won; and when we played 30 Seconds I always ended up in Donovan's team and he couldn't even draw a stickman. But Leila and her mum were odd. They didn't talk to each other much.

'I wonder what kind of dog it was,' said Mrs Merriman, who was still staring at the paw prints. She straightened up and rubbed her back. 'People don't realize how many homeless dogs roam this city. I sometimes wish they could be forced to visit the SPCA at least once a year – it breaks your heart. I don't know how anyone can just dump an animal.'

Mrs Merriman was sounding like her old self again this morning. It was the same little speech she always made when she came to our gate to collect money for the SPCA.

She spread her pink picnic blanket under the tree and sat down. George and Trixibelle were still sniffing around curiously, as if the patchy lawn was a dog newspaper full of juicy news items. Mrs Merriman made herself comfortable and took out her magazine.

For a while, all we heard were birds chirping and Mrs Merriman's pencil scribbling as she completed her crossword puzzle.

'Why pink?' asked Leila.

Mrs Merriman looked up in surprise. She stroked her pink hair, suddenly looking self-conscious, and a trace of sadness appeared around her mouth.

I couldn't believe that Leila had asked her something like that. I had often wondered why Mrs Merriman had pink hair and wore pink lipstick and pink clothes, but I had never considered asking her why.

She gave a funny little sigh and smiled. 'Why not pink?' she asked. 'All my life I had drab hair, wore drab clothes, worked in a drab office and lived in a drab house. I was even married to a drab man. So, now that I'm old and my husband is long dead, I wear pink.'

Suddenly George started to yap a short distance from us. The two sniffing doggies had wandered off from the tree and George was eyeing a thicket of shrubs suspiciously. He yapped again. Then Trixibelle let fly and started barking hysterically.

'Georgie! Trix!' called Mrs Merriman anxiously. 'Come here, my darlings! What's going on?'

She got up and went over to investigate.

A threatening growl was coming from the shrubs.

I'd once read in a magazine about wild animals, like hyenas and leopards, that prowled city streets at night and fed on leftovers in people's rubbish bins. What on earth was I going to do if a hyena or a leopard pounced on Mrs Merriman in broad daylight?

'Watch out, Mrs Merriman!' I warned.

She picked up George and Trixibelle and walked back to the tree.

'Stay here, doggies,' she said in a strict voice. Then she took something from the pink bag. She walked back to the shrubs. Obviously she had never read magazine articles about hyenas and leopards that ended up in cities.

'Come and see what I have,' she said, holding something in her outstretched hand. 'Don't worry,' she said soothingly. 'I'll just leave it here for you.'

She put a sandwich down on the ground and slowly backed off.

I gave Leila a quizzical look but she didn't seem to have a clue what was going on either.

Something moved inside the shrubs. I gasped in surprise. A large black dog appeared, its head close to the ground. First it glanced around suspiciously, then it made a dash for the sandwich and wolfed it down in a couple of greedy bites. The emaciated dog's ribs looked like they were about to poke through its skin.

'Look!' an astounded Leila said.

From among the shrubs a small puppy appeared clumsily on wobbly legs, followed by another one.

'Quiet, you two,' Mrs Merriman reprimanded when George and Trixibelle growled. She wiped her eyes as she watched the dog eating. 'You poor, poor thing.'

She rummaged in her bag for more sandwiches. When she approached them, the black dog backed off with her tail between her legs.

Mrs Merriman put the sandwiches down in the same spot and returned to us.

The big dog stole up to the sandwiches and started eating them.

Mrs Merriman stood under the tree and watched the dog gobbling up the food.

'When your hair's pink and you wear pink, you're noticed wherever you go,' she said in a strange voice. She stopped speaking and cleared her throat. 'I have a son but I don't know where he is. We haven't spoken to each other in years. He got involved with the wrong friends. Started stealing and using drugs; sometimes disappeared for weeks. I wanted to help him – that's why I had him admitted to a rehab centre – but he was furious with me. When he left rehab he disappeared without a trace. I don't know where he is. I don't know whether he even has a bed to sleep in at night. Maybe he's also sleeping under a bush in a park somewhere, like an abandoned dog. That's where I found him the last time, when I had him admitted to the rehab centre. I'm scared I might walk past him in the street one day and

we won't even notice each other...' She blew her nose.

Next to me Leila sniffed loudly. Tears were streaming down her cheeks. Without a word I passed her the kitchen dishcloth.

Mrs Merriman cleared her throat again. 'The two of you will have to excuse me today.' Suddenly her voice sounded normal again. 'I have to go and make arrangements for this poor dog and her puppies to be taken care of. Unfortunately I have no more sandwiches but I still have your cold drinks. Don't let that man from the municipality bully you! What you're doing here is a good thing. A good and a brave and a beautiful thing. Far too few good things are happening in the world.'

I stared after Mrs Merriman as she walked away. Leila's puffy eyes made me uncomfortable, so I preferred not to look at her.

I never knew what to do when girls cried. My mum wasn't like other mothers who cried at the movies. Maybe that was a good thing. Rohan, my best mate who had gone to America for the holidays, had a mother who cried about everything. She once burst into tears when our rugby team lost a match. For an entire week after that, Rohan seriously considered taking up chess.

It was starting to get warm. I stretched my legs and tried to make myself comfortable against the trunk of the tree.

'I wonder what that journalist is going to write about us in the paper?' I said to Leila.

She just shrugged.

'You don't even look glad about it,' I said. 'But my little brother actually did us a favour. If people read about the tree, we could have a better chance of saving it.'

I looked up.

Had I ever truly looked at a tree? All of a sudden, it felt as if I was looking at the trees in the park with new eyes. The tree we were sitting in was hardly ever quiet. The leaves kept rustling lightly, even if you couldn't feel the wind blowing, and they kept changing colour – greyish green, shiny green, khaki-green, shadowy green. Until the day before, I had never even known that white karee trees existed. Leila, on the other hand, could even remember the tree's scientific name.

'D'you know some other trees as well?' I asked.

Leila started to name all our tree's neighbours. 'Blue gum. Pine. White stinkwood. Sweet thorn. Cabbage tree.'

'How come you know all the names?' I asked.

Leila shrugged. 'It's just something I know.'

At lunchtime, Leila's mum brought us some sandwiches and fruit. I was happy for an excuse to climb down because it felt as if my backside had been chafed raw. When my grandfather was ill, I heard that you could get bedsores from lying in bed for too long. I wondered whether you could get tree-sores from sitting in a tree for too long.

Leila ate her sandwiches up in the tree. So far that day she had climbed down only once, to use the restroom at the bowling club.

After we'd eaten, Leila's mum sat down under the tree, read for a while and then went back home.

Leila and I remained in the tree, alone again. But not for long.

Soon I saw two children walking towards us. I groaned when I recognized Donovan's tilted cap and help-me-look-strong shirt, and Adrian's button-up shirt. My little brother refused to wear T-shirts – he was only nine years old but he dressed like an adult. A very boring adult. Apparently it had something to do with his business and the fact that he wanted people to take him seriously.

'Hey, tree-hugger,' Donovan said sneeringly.

'Hello, Donovan,' answered Leila cheerfully.

Donovan's cheeks went red. 'Sorry, I was actually speaking to that baboon,' he said.

I ignored him. 'Adrian, if Mum finds out that you called the paper and tried to make money from this, she's going to skin you alive and make some shoes so she can kick your arse.' It was the same creepy threat my mum always used when we'd been up to no good.

My little brother rolled his eyes. 'Who's going to tell her – you?'

'Maybe.'

'Don't forget you still owe me heaps of money.' He took something from his pocket. 'And I think you probably want this.' He triumphantly held my PSP in the air.

'That thing doesn't work anyway,' I said.

'I know someone who fixes electronic stuff,' he said. 'You owe me for that as well.'

'I didn't tell you to have it fixed,' I muttered.

But Adrian was one step ahead of me yet again – he obviously knew I was bored to death up there in the tree. In my little brother's mind even someone's boredom was an opportunity to make money.

'Mum told us to bring your toiletry bag,' said Donovan. 'This is the first and last time. Don't think I'm going to run after you every day just because you're sitting in a stupid tree.'

'What did Mum say when she got home last night?' I asked gingerly.

Donovan whistled through his teeth. 'Believe me, you don't want to know. All hell broke loose. Mum was worse than a T-rex with toothache. You'd better come home – you're messing up everyone's holiday.'

'I'm glad you're missing me that much,' I said sarcastically.

'C'mon, Adrian. I'm not going to stand here all day, yakking to our crazy brother in the tree,' said Donovan.

When they turned to leave, I quickly called, 'Adrian, wait! Erm...the PlayStation?'

My little brother grinned as he handed it over. I could pretty much see the dollar signs in his eyes, like in the comics.

After they'd left, I held the PSP out to Leila. 'You want to play?'

She smiled and shook her head. 'No, you go ahead.'

Adrian had put *Pro Evolution Soccer* into the PSP. Not my favourite but at least it would help pass the time.

And talking about time – thanks to the PSP, I could see what time it was. It was 3:17 and my team had just lost spectacularly against Brazil, when three municipal pickups stopped some distance from us.

I gave Leila a worried look.

Teams of workmen got off the pickups. Red-face started barking orders while Rat-face helped the workers to unload their equipment.

'Sweet thorn,' Leila said softly, as if it was a secret, magic word.

It took a moment before I realized it was the name of a tree. The tree the municipal workers had tackled.

A chainsaw started buzzing.

As if hypnotized, I sat watching as they cut down the tree. At first the chainsaw roared like a furious predator, and then there was an awful tearing sound, followed by a muffled thump. It looked as if a final shudder was going through the tree.

The air smelled of fresh sawdust. In the ensuing silence, not even one bird chirped.

I slowly breathed out and looked at Leila.

She was sitting there, staring into the distance as if she hadn't seen anything, but the white lines around her mouth told me that she was clenching her teeth.

When she looked at me, there were ice splinters in her blue eyes.

10

Milly

It was late evening. Our second night in the tree.

I yawned. Below us on the ground I could hear Leila's mum breathing peacefully. I wasn't sure how, but I just knew Leila was still awake too. It was as if I could sense that she was also listening to the sounds of the night. I leaned back against the rough trunk and looked at the stars that were slowly sliding by in between the leaves.

The Tree At The Centre Of The Universe, Leila had called it. I still didn't know what exactly she meant by that.

I wondered how Mrs Merriman and the big dog were doing. Around five that afternoon, she had showed up in the park with an SPCA van. They had come to fetch the dog and her puppies.

When Mrs Merriman saw that the sweet-thorn tree had been felled, she burst into tears.

It had been a day of tears. I hoped there would be less crying the following day.

It was quite a struggle to get the dog and her puppies into the van. She was really vicious when the people from the SPCA approached her. In the end they had to put a tranquillizer into a piece of meat, which they positioned near her hiding place.

I felt sorry for the poor drugged dog when she and her puppies were loaded into the van. What would become of them? I knew what usually happened to stray dogs that had no home, but this dog was a mummy dog...

At around seven thirty in the evening, my mum showed up again. This time she didn't fight. To tell you the truth, she barely said a word to me. She brought me a pillow, a tracksuit top, a large bottle of fruit juice and a container with meat pies from Woolworths. Then she left.

Leila and I scoffed the meat pies down cold. I wondered if Mum thought the average tree was equipped with a microwave oven.

'Milly,' Leila whispered as we sat on the ground.

'Huh?' I whispered back.

'The dog,' said Leila. 'Can we call her Milly?'

'Why not?' I said and shrugged. 'I mean, I don't think Mrs Merriman would mind.'

For some reason I felt proud that Leila had asked me for my opinion.

11

Green

The first thing I became aware of the next morning when I opened my eyes was that I was lying with my head on Leila's mum's shoulder. I wanted to die of shame but I remained lying like that, too scared to get up and wake her. Hopefully I hadn't snored or drooled on her shoulder in my sleep. Leila and I had swapped places just after midnight.

The second thing I became aware of was shreds of whispering voices.

'...really amazing...'

'...so cool...'

'...and they're still so young...'

'...most beautiful tree I've ever seen...'

'Marnus, wake up!'

The last voice was louder and belonged to Leila.

I sat up.

And my mouth fell open.

A little way from us I saw a group of people.

There were about fifteen of them, I guessed. Most of them were wearing weird, gaudy clothes. They stood there, looking at Leila and her mum and me as if we were exotic animals in a zoo. Next to me, Leila's mum woke with a startled 'huh?' and sat up.

A girl approached us. She looked like the leader of the group. The morning sun glistened on her dark brown, shaved scalp. She had three nose rings. I wondered if it hurt when she had her nostrils pierced.

'I'm Killer,' she said.

I swallowed. It's not every day that you meet a girl by the name of Killer on an empty stomach.

'Erm…I'm Marnus,' I said. Having just woken up, my voice still sounded tinny.

The group of people laughed as if I had made a joke.

'We know who you are, Marnus,' said Killer with a smile. 'We read about you and Leila in this morning's paper. You're very brave. We immediately decided to come and help you.'

'Help?' I asked.

'We're all students,' she said. 'And we've just finished writing exams. So we're going to give the two of you a hand.'

'Stop the fascists!' exclaimed one of the guys in the group, a redhead with wild dreadlocks, who held a poster up in the air. The poster said: *STOP THE FASCISTS!*

'Save our tree! Save our tree! Save our tree!' a girl started chanting. She sounded so angry that it made my stomach turn.

Anxiously, I glanced at Leila's mum. I had no idea what a fascist was but it didn't sound good.

'The tree must stay! The tree must stay!' Now the entire group of students was chanting.

Up in the tree, Leila sat as wide-eyed as a startled bushbaby. It looked like she didn't know what to think of Killer and the group of student demonstrators.

'Hold it!' bellowed a voice.

The chanting stopped.

Everyone looked at the caretaker in surprise. I was impressed with Uncle John's loud voice. He was standing with a tray in his hands, glowering at the students. 'What are you lot doing here?'

'We read in the paper about Leila and Marnus who're trying to save the tree,' said Killer. 'We decided to come and help them.' She looked the caretaker straight in the eye as she spoke. Her voice was calm but she sounded like someone who wouldn't mind fighting, if that was necessary.

Uncle John seemed to ponder this for a moment. Then he eyed the students, one after the other.

'All right,' he said with a sigh. 'I guess I can't stop you. But you're not allowed to use the restrooms at the bowling club. I don't want any trouble. Only Marnus and Leila are allowed there. And this isn't the local Mugg & Bean, so I didn't make coffee for all of you.'

Without a word, Leila's mum and I each took a mug of coffee. Leila clambered down and I carefully handed her the third mug.

'The tree must stay! The tree must stay!' the group of students started chanting again.

Uncle John gave me a folded newspaper. 'Some reading matter for you.'

I quickly swallowed my coffee, climbed into the tree and sat down next to Leila, who was already back up there. When I unfolded the paper my throat tightened. On the front page, just under the lead story, was a picture of Leila and me in the tree. It was taken from below, with our dangling feet filling almost the entire picture. The headline was: *Young friends go out on a limb for tree.*

I glanced at Leila. Were we friends? Before she rang our doorbell two mornings ago, I had never set eyes on her, even though we had been living only a couple of streets away from each other. Actually, I still knew very little about her.

'Right, I'm going to shower,' Leila's mum said. She glanced at the group of students and then gave us a worried look. 'Will you two be OK?'

'Yes, ma'am,' I said.

Leila just nodded.

The caretaker gestured with a thumbs up that she needn't worry.

I wondered why Leila didn't really speak to her mum. Had I been more like Leila, I would have asked her bluntly, 'What's going on between you and your mum?' – the way she'd asked Mrs Merriman, 'Why pink?' – but I was too shy.

After a while, Killer and the rest of the students seemed to realize that it was no use shouting 'The tree must stay!' and 'Stop the fascists!' when there were no fascists to shout at. They had moved aside and were sitting in the sun, smoking.

Sometime after the caretaker had left with the tray of coffee mugs, two municipal pickups and a smallish lorry approached. They stopped at the sweet thorn that had been felled.

Red-face got out of one of the pickups. Placing his hands on his hips, he looked at the chopped-down tree. Dew was glistening on the leaves that were now dull green and wilted. Workers in blue overalls descended on the tree.

'Front page, eh?' shouted Red-face at Leila and me. 'Don't think you being in the paper will save that tree. The town planners looked at the plans yesterday. The pipe has to pass through here. There's no other way.'

From where Red-face was standing, he obviously didn't see the students, so he staggered back a few steps when Killer and the others suddenly surrounded him.

They were waving their posters, chanting angrily, 'The tree must stay! Stop the fascists!'

Red-face wagged his finger at them but the chanting and the noise the workers were making with their chainsaws drowned out his voice.

I looked at Leila. It was difficult to guess what she was thinking. I'd expected that she would sit and watch all this with a satisfied smile but there was a small frown between her brows. You could see that her hair hadn't been close to a brush for the past two days. The tousled ponytail hung limp on her back.

I wished I could touch it.

That stupid thought made my face go all hot. I was sure that I looked like a thirteen-year-old version of Red-face for a moment.

The rest of that morning, the municipal workers were busy sawing up the tree and loading the pieces on to the lorry. They didn't seem very

bothered by the students waving posters around while shouting slogans and singing furious songs.

One of the girls recited a poem that she made up as she went along. At least, I thought she did because I didn't think anyone could learn a poem that long by heart. It was about a tree bleeding and a planet suffocating, and innocent women and children suffering due to war and violence. I actually didn't understand much of what she was saying but when she finished all the students applauded.

Cars in the street slowed down so that people could watch this spectacle, and every so often curious people approached to watch from up close. Some even chatted to Leila and me. They said things like:

'Hey, I saw you guys in the paper!'

'Where are your mothers and fathers? How can they allow you to stay up there?'

'Isn't that branch damn hard?'

'It's great that someone is doing something to preserve the planet.'

Around eleven, Junior du Toit showed up. He was wearing the same tight, bright-green pants and black and white sneakers as the previous day. First he took pictures of the group of students and the municipal workers, then he took up position under our tree.

'Did you see the article?' he asked and held a newspaper out to us.

I nodded.

'I hope you liked it.' He smiled in his beard and pointed towards the students. 'Seems like you grabbed people's attention. I'm going to write a follow-up for tomorrow's paper. But tell me: how are you guys feeling this morning?'

I waited for Leila to say something but she just stared straight ahead of her.

'Well…my bum is hurting a bit,' I said.

Immediately I felt like an idiot. Donovan and Adrian would kill themselves laughing if that was to appear in the morning paper.

'But…erm…it's for a good cause,' I said. 'We're not going to give up hope. We're going to stay here until the tree is saved.'

That sounded more like something that should be quoted in a newspaper article.

Junior asked some more questions. I tried my best to give clever answers. I wished I could see what he was writing in his notebook.

At last, he was satisfied. He took more pictures of Leila and me, and then he walked off.

When Junior had left, I gave Leila a dirty look.

'Why were you just sitting there, letting me answer all the questions?'

She simply shrugged. There were dark circles under her eyes. She'd slept much less than I had the past two nights.

Suddenly I thought of something.

'Leila, are you tired of this tree thing?' I asked. 'I mean, if you want to go home, just say. Those students are here now and it's been in the paper and everything...'

Without a word, Leila picked up the kitchen dishcloth that she had used the previous day to wipe her tears and held it out to me.

'You can go if you want,' she said softly. 'Nothing's keeping you here.'

'That's not what I meant!' I quickly defended myself. 'I was just checking in case I was sitting in this tree thinking *you* wanted me to stay here, and you were just sitting here because you thought *I* wanted to stay here. I mean, that would be bloody stupid.'

Leila gave me a piercing look. She was good at that.

Maybe, I thought, *she'll become a lawyer like my mum*. My mum always said a stern look in court was sometimes worth much more than a whole speech.

I looked away. I didn't feel like listening to the long speech in Leila's eyes.

12

The Fight

By late afternoon, Killer and the group of students seemed tired of shouting slogans and waving posters around. The municipal pickups and lorry had left about an hour before that with the chopped-up tree.

The students made themselves comfortable a little way off under a blue gum tree. Thanks to Leila, I was becoming something of a tree expert.

We sat in the tree and watched the students light a fire and laugh and chat around it. The guy with the red dreadlocks and one of the girls, a blonde with long hair, were obviously terribly in love. They sat on the grass and were kissing each other as if they'd forgotten about the people around them. I wondered if that was the way Donovan kissed the girls in the *lapa*. He had threatened to kill me deader than dead if I dared come close while he was giving kissing lessons.

I stole a quick glance at Leila. She was sitting there with a strange little smile as she watched the two lovers kissing non-stop.

Donovan was barely two years older than me but he was an expert kisser. I, on the other hand, had never kissed a girl properly. OK, there was that one time at Rohan's birthday party when his cousin kissed me while we were both hiding in the wardrobe, but that was only a quick peck – and afterwards I found out that she had kissed almost all the guys at the party. I was thinking of a real kiss – the kind that smudged a girl's lipstick and messed up her hair and made her cheeks glow.

When dusk fell, a brightly painted kombi parked under the blue gum tree. More students poured out of it. They greeted Killer's little group noisily and started to unload cooler boxes from the kombi.

'You know I don't eat meat,' grumbled the girl who had recited the poem. 'I can't believe you're such barbarians. How can you eat something that had a face?' She looked very upset. I really hoped she wouldn't rattle off a new poem about people who ate meat.

Someone said something and everyone laughed.

Thanks to Mrs Merriman, we had had roast beef, baked potatoes, beans and pumpkin for lunch. She had passed by earlier that afternoon with dishes filled to the brim in her pink picnic bag. 'Young children need healthy, traditional country cooking,' she said and gave the containers of Woolworths food that my dad had delivered a disapproving look.

Mrs Merriman hadn't said much about the group of students. While we ate, she just watched them in silence. I wondered if she was thinking of her son.

My dad also didn't have much to say when he was here; he just stared at Leila and me up in the tree and shook his head as if he was watching a rugby game in which the ref kept making bad decisions.

However, Mrs Merriman did tell us that the big dog and her puppies were doing well. She thought Milly was a very pretty name and promised to tell the SPCA people to call her that. Mrs Merriman and the SPCA would try very hard to find them all a good home.

When dusk turned into night, Leila's mum switched on a small battery-powered lantern. I wondered if she had gone off specially to buy it, as the wind had blown the candles out the previous nights.

The students laughed and chatted louder and louder. They sat in a small circle in the yellow light of the fire, almost all of them with a bottle in their hand. It looked strange in the dark – our white lantern circle and their orangey-yellow fire circle.

'Are the three of you OK here?' asked a voice. The rings in Killer's nose glimmered in the light of the lantern.

'All good, thank you,' said Leila's mum. Her voice sounded a little strange – slightly anxious.

Killer looked up to where Leila and I were sitting on the branch in the dark. 'Sorry about the noise,' she said. 'That lot will use any excuse to party.'

Leila and her mum said nothing. I knew it was because they didn't want to say anything. It was something they often did.

The only reason I wasn't saying anything was because I couldn't think of anything to say.

'I really think you're very brave,' said Killer.

I felt sorry for her because no one was saying anything.

'Erm...I think it was very brave to have those rings put in your nose,' I said. 'It must've hurt.' That was probably a stupid thing to say but at least it was something.

She laughed. 'It hurt my mum and dad more than it hurt me.'

I didn't really understand what she meant, so I couldn't think of anything else to say.

Killer stayed with us for a moment then walked back to the fire.

Leila climbed down and went to sit with her mum. They didn't talk.

I was bored, so I grabbed the PlayStation and played for a while with the volume louder than necessary. I wasn't sure what was getting on my nerves most – the noisy students or the silence under the tree.

By the time the PlayStation's battery became flat, one of the students had got hold of a guitar. They sat in a circle in the dark and sang songs I didn't know.

A girl brought Leila and her mum and me a paper plate each with a sausage and a vegetable kebab. Leila gave me hers.

I took a bite or two. The kebab tasted of smoke and the sausage was still raw. If Milly had been here, I wouldn't have minded giving her mine.

I suddenly wondered what kind of tree had been chopped down for the firewood that the students used. Did any of them ever think of that? It was quite a depressing thought.

Leila climbed up and sat next to me again. 'You can go and sleep if you want,' she said.

I shrugged. 'I'm not really sleepy yet.'

I looked down. Leila's mum was lying on a

duvet, with her back to us. I wasn't sure whether she was sleeping.

'Why did you decide to call the dog Milly?' I asked.

'Milly was my first dog,' she said. 'My... erm...I got her when I was very small. She was run over by a car when I was ten. I never wanted another dog again.'

'We have a dog,' I said. 'Mr Bones. He's a real mutt. He sort of belongs to all of us. My brothers and I fight about who has to pick up the turds on the lawn.'

Leila laughed.

It was weird: every time she laughed, I couldn't help smiling. I thought she laughed far too seldom.

Slowly but surely, the voices of the students grew silent. The guitar was put away and all that remained was the faint glow of the fire.

Then two of them started fighting.

I could only hear bits of the fight but I recognized the voices. It was the guy with the red dreadlocks and his girlfriend. They had obviously forgotten about their passionate kissing earlier.

'...said you'd go on holiday with me...'

'...promised my parents...'

'...don't really feel anything for me...'

'...know that isn't true...sometimes be so childish...'

Their voices got louder and louder in the dark.

'You're just like my dad!' the girl shouted and started crying.

Unexpectedly, I felt Leila's hand creeping over mine, like a frightened, warm little animal. There was a buzzing noise in my ears.

The guy screamed something at the girl.

Suddenly a bright light went on.

'Enough of this,' said a voice. The caretaker didn't raise his voice but immediately there was a hushed silence. 'Have you no shame? How can you carry on like that in front of two children! Is one of you still sober enough to drive this kombi? I hope so, because if you're still here by tomorrow morning there'll be trouble.'

'Hey, Grandpa, who made you head boy?' asked the guy with the dreadlocks.

'Shut up.' Killer's no-nonsense voice cut through the dark.

The guy kept quiet.

'Put out that fire,' the caretaker continued. 'Didn't you see the notice that prohibits the lighting of fires in the park? What's the use of protesting to save the trees while you're trying your best to burn the place down?'

There was a guilty silence, like straight after a teacher had told off a noisy class.

The torchlight shone up into the tree.

Embarrassed, I wriggled my hand out from under Leila's. I blinked in the blinding light.

'Are you OK?' asked the caretaker.

'Yes. Thanks a lot,' said Leila. She sounded really relieved.

Leila's mum folded her arms around her body as if she was cold. 'I wish we could just go home,' she said. It sounded like she was talking to herself.

The caretaker lowered the torch and came closer, until he was standing under the tree. His voice sounded tired when he spoke. 'I know it's not for me to say but you can't cling to one tree for ever. Not even a good tree like this one.'

I wasn't sure what he actually meant, but I did know that he wasn't speaking to me. I was almost certain he was trying to tell Leila something.

He leaned with his back against the tree trunk and the torch threw a yellow circle of light on the ground by his feet.

'I told you about my brother, the one who lay down in front of the bulldozers when they started to demolish District Six,' he spoke into the darkness. 'My little brother was brave. I was proud of him. But after that he got angrier and angrier. He was angry at the government. Angry at white people. Angry at my mother and the people who didn't try to fight back. Angry because he had to go and live in a different house and go to a different school.

'I tried to talk to him but his anger made him deaf. He dropped out of school and started to fight against the apartheid government.' Uncle John sighed. 'And he lost. He died in the police cells. Back then, that's how things went down. It's good to fight for something but you also have to know when to stop – otherwise the fight can become bigger than the thing you're fighting against.'

It was silent as the grave. I wondered if the students had also listened to the caretaker's story.

Without another word, he straightened up and walked off into the dark, the circle of light bobbing about in front of him.

The story he had just told us was still ringing in my ears, the way the chainsaws did when the municipal workers had finally switched them off.

I knew there was a reason why he'd told us that story but my brain felt too tired to figure it out.

In the dark I could hear the students whisper as if they were also trying to work out what had just happened.

I wished Leila would say something.

13

The Heart of a Tree

In the middle of the night, a rustling sound woke me. I opened my eyes and pricked up my ears, but I didn't move or get up from the ground. The park was dead quiet.

In the faint moonlight I saw Leila get down from the tree. Maybe she wanted to go to the loo. I probably should have offered to walk with her in the dark but I decided to wait for a moment. When she was on the ground, she cautiously looked in my direction. I didn't move.

Earlier in the year, our class had gone on a Zoo Snooze. There were special red lights in the cages of the nocturnal animals so we could watch them as they moved about. Leila moved as agilely and softly as a genet in the dark. She went silently over to her mum. Gently, she got hold of the corner of the blanket and pulled it over her mum, who stirred slightly in her sleep. Leila squatted next to her. It was difficult to see exactly what she was doing but it looked as if she was just sitting there, staring at her mum. She remained like that for quite a while before she raised her hand and stroked her mum's hair. Then she got up.

'Marnus,' she whispered to me. 'Come.'

I gasped. How did she know that I was awake?

Without a word, I followed her back up the tree.

My bum must have grown accustomed to sitting uncomfortably because I quickly eased into my usual position on the branch.

When both of us were seated, Leila switched on a torch. That afternoon her mum had remembered to bring a torch from home but I hadn't seen Leila bring it into the tree with her.

I took a deep breath and before I could stop myself, I asked the question that had been bugging me for the past three days. It was probably the most obvious question to ask when you spend three nights in a tree with someone, but until that moment I hadn't mustered the courage to do so.

'Leila,' I whispered, 'why are you really doing this?'

'What?' she asked.

'You know what I mean.' I knew she was acting dumb on purpose. 'The tree…Why *this* tree? Why not the sweet thorn or one of the blue gums or the white stinkwood?'

'I've told you already,' said Leila.

'Because this was the first tree you learned to climb?' I asked. 'Because it's…The Tree At The Centre Of The Universe?'

Leila leaned back against the tree trunk.

'You're stranded on an island and you have only three things with you,' she said, ignoring my question. I had noticed that she was quite good at that. 'A kitchen dishcloth, a torch and a packet of raisins. What would you do with them?'

I heard plastic tear and she held a packet of raisins out to me.

I took a handful. 'You think cannibals will eat raisins?' I asked.

'Maybe,' she said. 'If you can convince them that they're dried eyeballs or something like that.'

I laughed.

When she spoke again, her voice was a mere whisper. 'My dad came up with the island game. It eats up boring kilometres when you're on a long road trip. My island always had cannibals and I always used my three things to become a cannibal princess. When it was my mum's turn, George Clooney always showed up miraculously to save her, and then she'd use her three things to make life on the island as much fun as possible for him. My dad always pretended that it made him terribly jealous. He always used his three things to make incredibly clever and weird plans to get home again.'

'Your dad...?' I asked cautiously.

'He taught me how to climb a tree,' she said. 'He always said we have baboon blood in our veins. In the evenings before bedtime we sometimes came to play here in the park and then we'd climb to the top of the tree and he'd show me the stars and tell me stories of cannibal princesses and dragons and mermaids, and wild girls with baboon blood, and trees that can walk and talk.'

I didn't ask any more questions, because she seemed to be speaking to herself.

'Want to see something?' she asked.

I nodded, slightly surprised that she knew I was still there.

She handed me the torch. Then she got to her feet on the branch.

'Watch out,' I said. If she fell, she would break her neck.

'Shine over here,' she said and pushed a branch aside.

I searched with the torch until I found the spot she was indicating. I was surprised to see that something had been carved into the bark

– there were reddish-brown cuts in the dark trunk. Carefully I straightened myself on the branch to see better.

It was a heart.

It looked like someone had carved it with a pocketknife. It seemed like the deep cuts in the trunk had healed a long time ago. Something was written inside the heart.

W + M

'This only became my tree for climbing later on,' said Leila. 'Before I was born, this was my mum and dad's tree. He carved these letters for her.'

'Leila?' asked a sleepy voice from below us.

I got such a fright that I nearly lost my balance.

'Is everything OK?'

'We're OK, ma'am,' I answered shakily.

A panicked thought crossed my mind: *what if Leila's mum thinks we're busy with...well... kissing lessons?*

I sank back on to the branch.

Leila switched off the torch. It took a while for my eyes to get used to the dark again. Above us stars were peeping through the leaves here and there.

'My dad dumped my mum.' Leila's voice was just a whisper. 'For another woman.'

14

Tree Children

By dawn the next morning, most of the students had left in their kombi. All that remained was the greyish-black spot where they had made their fire the evening before, and three khaki-green sleeping-bag caterpillars on the grass. The three students who remained behind had crawled so deep into their sleeping bags that I couldn't see who they were. The posters they had been waving around the day before were leaning against the blue gum.

I stretched my legs and looked at Leila and her mum, who were lying under the tree, still fast asleep.

The conversation Leila and I had had the previous night felt like a dream but when I looked up through the thick leaves I could see the tip of the heart on the tree trunk.

I thought of my mum and dad. They were forever fighting. In my mind I tried to make a list of ten things they had been arguing about during the past week or so:

1 The new signage that Dad wanted to put up at the sports shop. (Mum: 'That kind of thing costs a fortune. Your finances are looking dire enough already.')

2 The fact that the sports shop's finances were looking so dire. (Dad: 'It's because our sign is too small. People walk right past the shop without seeing it.')

3 The motor of the electric gate in our driveway that had conked out.

4 Empty beer cans in front of the TV.

5 Donovan's school report.

6 The fact that my dad had borrowed money from Adrian to order pizza.

7 A turkey. (Mum: 'OK, if you want to eat turkey on Christmas Day, go ahead and buy one and start stuffing it, because I certainly won't be. Obviously no one in this house has any appreciation whatsoever of the fact that I'm busy with a Very Important Court Case.')

8 The fact that my mum was so busy with her Very Important Court Case.

9 Who the best newsreader on TV was.

Before I could think of a tenth thing, I saw the caretaker approaching from the bowling green.

Exactly like the previous two mornings, he had a tray with coffee mugs in his hands. And exactly like the previous day, he was pinching a newspaper under one of his arms.

Maybe it was the smell of morning coffee that woke Leila and her mum, because by the time Uncle John had put the tray down under the tree they were both on their feet.

'Morning,' said the caretaker. His voice was light and happy, as if he had forgotten the horrible story he had told us the previous evening about his brother. 'I brought the three of you some coffee too!' he shouted towards the sleeping students.

The sleeping-bag caterpillars started to stir. First Killer's head popped out from one of the sleeping bags, and next to her two other girls were sitting up. One of them was the girl who'd fought with the red-headed guy. They scrambled out of their sleeping bags, joined us, stifling yawn after yawn, and gratefully accepted a mug of coffee each.

'Actually, I only drink organic coffee...' one girl said but then gave the caretaker a somewhat apprehensive look. 'But this smells delicious,' she quickly added.

Rather stiffly, I got out of the tree.

Seven mugs of coffee were steaming in the early-morning air.

'Sorry about last night,' said Killer.

I wasn't sure who she was apologizing to.

'What's your real name?' asked Leila in that strange, out-of-the-blue way of hers.

Killer choked on her coffee and looked at her wide-eyed. 'Who says Killer isn't my real name?'

Leila shrugged. 'You also started out as a baby. Who calls a little baby Killer?'

Killer's nose rings flashed in the morning sun. She looked up into the tree as if she had forgotten her real name and was hoping that it would be carved somewhere on the trunk. 'My real name is Joy,' she said. 'Joy Meintjies. And you're right. My mum and dad are teachers – they would never have called their little girl Killer.'

I stared at Killer. Or Joy. I couldn't decide which name suited her best. You could see she was trying to look like Killer but it felt to me as if she could be a Joy as well.

'But little girls grow up,' said Killer. Again I wasn't sure which of us she was addressing. 'And I guess sometimes they turn out different from what everyone had hoped.'

'Did you really kill someone?' asked Leila.

'Leila!' scolded her mum.

Killer laughed. 'Not yet,' she said and raised one eyebrow in a mock threat. 'I only killed my mum and dad's dream. A real killjoy, that's me.

The Morning News

MORE SUPPORT FOR TREE CHILDREN'S PROTEST

They had other plans for me, and I spoilt their fun. Actually, that's what my name should be: Killjoy.'

The caretaker cleared his throat. 'Well, I hate to be the killjoy now but I have to get to work. Here's the paper. I suspect you're going to have a busy day.'

He gave the newspaper to Leila and started collecting the empty coffee mugs.

My mouth dropped open when I saw the front page. The headline read: *More support for tree children's protest.*

Under the headline was a photo of the students demonstrating under the tree.

'*Facebook and Twitter are buzzing about the two children who are trying to save a tree in their local park*,' I read out loud. '*By last night a Facebook group that had been started in support of the two green soldiers already had more than 3,000 members. Also thanks to the two children, a stray dog and her puppies were discovered and subsequently saved by the SPCA.*'

I looked at Leila. She shuddered slightly and I didn't understand why.

15

The Best of Mother Earth

The first people to show up, at eight that morning, were a man and a woman wearing garish clothes and headbands in their long hair. They waved at us merrily and made themselves comfortable on the grass, a little way from Leila's mum's blanket. They looked up at Leila and me, and smiled as if they expected us to start giving a concert up in the tree at any moment.

Hot on their heels was a group of five cyclists with sunglasses and tanned calves. They propped their bikes up against the blue gum, next to the students' posters, and stood around chatting while gesturing towards us. One of them took a picture of us with his mobile phone.

'Oh no,' groaned Leila.

More and more people were arriving.

People walking their dogs.

Mothers with prams.

Joggers.

A choir started singing 'Joy to the World' and 'Away in a Manger'. The choir mistress had a sign around her neck that said they needed money for their overseas tour the next year, and in front of them on the lawn was a jar in which people could drop money.

A man with a Santa Claus hat.

Someone from a radio station.

An ice-cream seller on a bicycle.

Killer and the two students started handing out posters.

Before long, the choir switched from Christmas carols to singing: 'The tree must stay! The tree must stay!'

More coins tinkled in the donation jar.

A pink lady with two poodles was struggling to make her way through the crowd.

'Good grief, this looks like a church fete!' Mrs Merriman called out. She was the only one who dared come close to us; the others all kept a polite distance. 'Good morning, you two,' she greeted us, slightly out of breath.

She and George and Trixibelle settled in next to Leila's mum on one of the blankets.

'Gosh, look at all the people. Marnus, Leila, the two of you are becoming famous!'

She took a Tupperware container out of her

bag and opened it. It was full of muffins. She offered Leila and her mum and me some.

'You know, Milly and her pups are doing very well,' Mrs Merriman said. 'Milly seems to like her new name a lot. You should think of names for the puppies as well. After the story in this morning's paper, loads of people will call the SPCA and offer to take in Milly and her little ones and give them good homes.'

The crowd around the tree grew even larger. By ten o'clock it looked as if there was a flea market in the park.

When Leila wasn't looking, I tried my best to wet my hair from my water bottle and comb it, even though I didn't have a mirror. Imagine having to go on a stage and stand in front of 107 people without having combed your hair, washed your face or brushed your teeth! A few minutes ago, Mrs Merriman had tried to count the people and that's what she got: 107.

The tree felt increasingly like a stage, with Leila and me in the leading roles, even though we had no idea what to say or do.

It looked like Leila was starting to get stage-fright. She was biting on her bottom lip and staring intently at the branch in front of her.

Until then I had always been the dancing gnome or the innkeeper in school concerts. I had

never been given an important role. This was the first time I knew what it was like to feel everyone's eyes on me.

When Junior du Toit arrived to take pictures of us again, I grinned and pumped my fist in the air like the demonstrating students. I thought that would look cool in a photo.

Leila sat as if carved from stone.

By 11 A.M., Donovan arrived. He had a girl with him I had never seen before. She was incredibly pretty. She had dark hair, and her legs were long and tanned. They struggled to get through the people and reach the tree. I saw Donovan gesturing at Leila and me.

The girl smiled and waved at us. 'Is this really your brother?' she shouted at me over the singing students and choir, and pointed at Donovan.

I nodded.

The girl looked surprised, grinned and took Donovan's hand. 'I'm Melissa!' she called at me.

I waved to her. 'Hi, Melissa!'

Everyone looked at my brother and the girl.

Donovan grinned as if he had just won the Lotto. It looked like he would have only one student coming to his kissing lessons for the rest of the holidays.

'I have to go to the toilet,' I said to Leila when my brother and his girlfriend walked off.

She just shrugged as if to say, *So? Go. Does it look like I'm trying to stop you?*

Feeling offended, I took my toiletry bag and started climbing down. Why was Leila in such a weird mood?

'What's going on?' a worried voice shouted when I reached the ground.

Suddenly, the students and the choir stopped singing.

'Oh no, is that little boy giving up?' asked a lady with a grocery bag in her hand.

'Don't worry. He just needs to leave the tree...to take a leak!' someone else called.

Laughter rippled through the group of people.

My ears were burning. I walked off as fast as possible towards the bowling green.

There were no players on the green yet. I slipped in at the gate. There was no sign of the caretaker.

The restroom was cool and rather dark. I switched on the light and closed the door behind me. I could no longer hear the singing around the tree.

After doing my business, I stood in front of the washbasin and looked at myself in the mirror. My hair was all over the place, exactly as I had suspected. I opened the tap and held my head under the streaming water. Then I rubbed my hair dry with one of the small sparkling-white towels and tamed the worst cowlicks with my comb. I hung the towel neatly back on the rail and brushed my teeth.

When I was done, I dawdled a bit in the restroom. I thought maybe that was how an actor felt during the interval before the next act started, or a famous rock singer before having to go on stage.

I zipped up my toiletry bag, took one last look in the mirror and winked at myself.

Then I opened the bathroom door – and bumped into a man who came rushing in.

'Marnus!' He sounded concerned. 'Are you OK?'

'Sorry,' I muttered as my hand flew up to my stinging nose. My eyes began to water.

I didn't really know why I said sorry – after all, I was the one who got hurt. I cautiously touched my nose. Fortunately it didn't feel as if it was broken and it wasn't bleeding either.

The man held his hand out to me. 'You're just the guy I was hoping to bump into!' he said jokingly. 'Dimitri Giorgiou. Pleased to meet you.'

I shook his hand. My eyes were still watering a little from being hit on the nose.

The man who was shaking my hand had dark hair and a stubbly beard, but not the kind of creepy tramp stubble that my dad sported during holidays when he refused to shave – this guy had stubble like the male models in aftershave ads. I wondered whether he was hot in his suit but it looked as if he had just stepped out of an air-conditioned office.

'Hot, eh?' he asked, as if he could read my mind. 'How about a cold drink?'

He shoved a canary-yellow can into my hand.

I looked at it in surprise. My mum had told us a thousand times not to accept gifts from strangers.

'Er...no, thanks,' I said.

'Come on!' he said with a broad smile. 'Surely a man gets thirsty when he sits in a tree all day? I just want to say, I think what you and that girl are doing is absolutely fantastic. Green issues are on everyone's lips these days but few people are actually prepared to do something about global warming and pollution and the disappearance of our forests. That's why I'd like to be your sponsor.'

I frowned. Dimitri Giorgiou spoke so fast that my head was spinning.

'Sponsor?' I asked.

'That's right, yes.' He pointed at the can. 'What you're holding in your hand isn't just another ordinary cool drink. Let's start with the can – it's made of one hundred percent recycled metal. Minimum damage to the environment. But wait until you open it...'

He looked at me expectantly.

I opened the can.

The man kept looking at me, so I carefully took a sip – even though my mum would have had a fit.

'What does it taste like?' Dimitri asked.

Before I could decide if it would be rude to say it tasted a bit like cheap cordial that was too weak, the man answered his own question.

'It tastes like the best Mother Earth has to offer. That's where the name comes from – Nature's Gift. It's good for nature and it's good for you. No preservatives. No artificial flavouring or colourants. No extra sugar.'

I suspected all those things he had just mentioned were exactly what made ordinary cool drinks so great but I kept quiet.

'I have a proposition for you,' said the man. 'One you definitely can't say no to...'

16

Run

'I have good news,' I told Leila when I got back into the tree, slightly out of breath.

Getting from the bowling green to the tree took quite an effort. By then there really were a lot of people. Some of them stopped me to speak to me. A girl even asked for my autograph. She was quite pretty too. I thought Donovan would be jealous if I asked her for her mobile number.

Leila seemed not to have heard me over the crowd's noisy chattering and singing.

'I said, I have good news!' I said louder.

Leila didn't react – she just stared into nothingness. She didn't even notice my T-shirt. I was about to repeat myself even louder when she turned to me.

'He's here,' she said. It looked as if she had just heard that someone was on their way to flatten the tree with a bulldozer, the way they had demolished Uncle John's parents' house in District Six.

I frowned. 'Who?'

She was staring off into the distance again.

Confused, I looked at the people in the park. I reckoned there were about two hundred of them now, but oddly enough, my eyes were immediately drawn to a man at the back with blond hair. He was standing on the edge of the crowd. He was the only one who wasn't singing or chatting or gesturing wildly. His shoulders were slightly hunched as if he was carrying a heavy load, and he stood with his hands in the pockets of his three-quarter pants, staring at us. Something about his face, and his intent gaze, seemed familiar to me. I looked at Leila again.

'Is that...?' I started to ask.

But before I could continue, Dimitri Giorgiou approached us. Under his arm was a rolled-up banner. He unrolled it and used rope to tie it around the trunk of the tree.

'Hey, what do you think you're doing?' Mrs Merriman called, sounding annoyed.

George and Trixibelle growled.

'From now on, Nature's Gift is the official sponsor of The Tree At The Centre Of The Universe,' Dimitri announced in a proud voice. 'We're going to help save this tree. Nature's Gift is a refreshing, one hundred percent natural soft drink, free of any preservatives or...'

'What's he talking about?' Leila asked me. 'How does he know about The Tree At The Centre Of The Universe?'

She sounded quite calm but I still wasn't sure whether that was a good sign or not.

'That's what I wanted to tell you!' I said. 'We now have a sponsor.'

It felt surprisingly good to say that. My dad sponsored Donovan and the rest of the first team's rugby togs, and a well-known manufacturer of swimming trunks had offered to sponsor Donovan the following year when he competed in the national swimming championships. No one had ever offered to sponsor me for anything.

At that moment I felt far from invisible.

'Dimitri – that's the guy putting up the banner – is going to pay for pamphlets so that people can force the municipality to leave the tree alone and save this park,' I explained in one long, breathless sentence. I held one of the yellow T-shirts out to Leila. 'Look – this is your T-shirt. Dimitri is going to give all the people in the park one of these. I...'

Leila slapped the T-shirt out of my hand. It fell on to the ground like a dead canary. Her eyes were icy blue.

'What's with you?' I asked, surprised. 'I thought...Hey, where are you going?'

Leila started climbing down.

'Leila, come back!'

She didn't bother climbing down the last bit and just jumped to the ground.

Surprised, Dimitri Giorgiou stepped back when she landed next to him. The people close to the tree gasped and the ones behind tried to push each other out of the way to see what was going on.

Leila started to run.

'Leila?' her mum called. 'Leila!'

But it seemed Leila wasn't seeing or hearing anything. She stormed into the crowd. Taken aback, they made way for her. Leila's hair was flying behind her.

She ran past Killer and the choir members.

She ran past the ice-cream cart.

She ran over the road. A car hooted and tyres screeched on the tarmac.

She ran until I could no longer see her.

Slowly but surely, the people turned around. It felt as if everyone's eyes were burning a hole through me.

I swallowed.

It was as if a bulldozer had just run me over.

Slowly, I started climbing down.

My hand slipped and I scraped my leg raw on the tree bark. There were more shocked gasps from the onlookers.

I clenched my teeth, and when I got to the bottom I took a deep breath.

For a moment I looked at Mrs Merriman and Leila's mum.

I pulled the stupid yellow T-shirt with the Nature's Gift logo over my head and chucked it aside.

With my head hanging, I started walking home.

17

When Everything Changes *and* Stays Exactly the Same

'Hey, doofus, are you going to make me coffee or d'you want a wedgie?'

When someone says something like that to you, there are a couple of things you can do:

Option one: you can drop everything and immediately switch on the kettle.

Option two: you can point out to the person, in a very friendly manner, that you're busy doing the dishes because you owe your little brother more or less a year's pocket money, and tell him to make his own coffee.

Donovan's eyes widened when he heard my answer. He obviously hadn't expected me to choose option two.

'What did you say?' he hissed.

I chucked some knives and forks into the foaming dishwashing water. 'I said, make your own bloody coffee – unless you'd rather do the dishes yourself.'

Donovan approached me, looking threatening, then grinned unexpectedly. 'Playing hard-ass, eh?' He punched my shoulder but then, wonder of wonders, reached out and switched on the kettle. 'Don't think that just because you're going to high school next year and you spent a few days sitting in a tree with your girlfriend, you can suddenly do whatever you want. Do you get me?'

'She's not my girlfriend.'

My throat tightened when I thought of Leila.

This time the previous morning, everything had been different.

This time the previous morning, we were still sitting in the tree.

The caretaker had brought us coffee.

The students and the choir had sung songs and waved posters around.

People had taken photos of us.

And I had behaved like an idiot.

'Heard anything from her since?' asked Donovan.

I put a plate on the drying rack and looked at him in surprise. I couldn't remember my brother ever speaking to me as if I was a normal human being. Usually he only threatened me and made fun of me, always looking for a fight.

'Nope,' I said.

Donovan smiled. 'Girls are weird. You'll have to get used to it.' He checked his reflection in the oven door and flexed his biceps. 'Melissa goes on and on about global warming and the forests that are being chopped down and stuff like that. She thinks you and that Leila chick were terribly brave. She calls you ego-warriors, or something.'

'Eco-warriors,' I corrected him.

'What?'

I shook my head. 'Never mind.'

He rolled his eyes. 'Whatever. I still think it's stupid to sit in a tree for so long.' Donovan was quiet for a moment and started playing with the salt and pepper pots. It looked like he was making the two pots kiss each other. 'I told Dad I won't be playing rugby next year,' he said without looking up.

I nearly dropped a plate. 'You what?'

Donovan shrugged. 'I told him I'm going to focus on swimming instead.'

'What did he say?' I asked.

Even before Donovan was born, my dad had bought him his first rugby ball. If the first team played during shop hours sometimes Dad simply closed the sports shop. He never, ever missed one of Donovan's games.

'He didn't exactly do somersaults of joy,' Donovan said drily and sat on a kitchen chair, making himself comfortable by resting his bare feet on the table. 'But I think he was a little distracted by all the commotion you caused. Maybe it'll only sink in properly later.'

Maybe Dad felt the same way I did – as if everything that had happened in the past few days still had not sunk in properly. I guessed anyone would feel that way if one morning they opened the front door and, before they knew it, they were sitting up in a tree with a girl, and the two of you met all kinds of strange people and suddenly made the front page of the newspaper.

Yesterday afternoon, when I got home, I had collapsed on my bed and fallen asleep almost immediately. It had felt as if my brain had had enough of everything and decided to switch off. I only woke up when my mum called me for dinner.

We ate dinner as if nothing had happened. Mum talked about her Very Important Court Case. Dad complained about his shop's Christmas sales – which were looking dismal – and people preferring to slouch in front of the TV instead of exercising. Donovan was rather quiet – I suspected he was thinking of Melissa the whole time.

Adrian was the only one who kept asking questions about my three days in the tree. I answered as few of them as possible. Adrian was disappointed that I didn't ask the fruit-juice man for more money.

Outside the pool pump was going *chug-chug-chug.*

The fridge hummed like a purring cat.

At the front gate Mr Bones was barking at the reverend's wife, who walked past with her German shepherd, as she usually did that time of the morning.

It felt as if I had been in a time machine and had gone back three days...

Mrs Merriman, who wore pink and missed her son who wandered the streets.

Milly and her puppies.

The caretaker and the story about the bulldozers.

The bowls players practising being angels.

Killer, whose real name was Joy.

The front-page articles.

The island game.

Leila and The Tree At The Centre Of The Universe, with her dad and mum's initials carved into the trunk.

It felt as if all those things had been merely a dream.

It felt as if something had changed during the past three days.

Yet everything suddenly felt exactly the same again.

I was so freaking lost in thought that I accidentally made Donovan coffee when the kettle boiled, even though I had convinced him for the very first time in my life to do it himself.

18

An Invisible Tree

Late that afternoon, I went to the park.

'Where are you going?' a suspicious Donovan wanted to know when he saw me sneaking out the front door. 'Mum said I had to make sure you don't get up to something crazy again.'

I promised him I wasn't planning to go and sit in the tree.

The park was deserted when I got there.

Everyone had left. Killer and the students. The choir. The cyclists. The pretty girl who had asked for my autograph.

And the tree.

The municipality had been there. Red-face and Rat-face had done their job.

In a way I had expected that but it was still a shock to see the stump sticking out of the ground.

Once, when I was seven or eight years old, I was in the play area at McDonald's and I saw a woman who had no arm, only a stump. The

141

woman must have seen me staring at it because she walked up to me and asked with a friendly smile, 'Do you want to feel it?' I got such a fright that I started to cry hysterically and ran away to my parents. For weeks afterwards I had nightmares about the woman's pink stump.

That was what the tree stump looked like – like something you couldn't stop staring at but that you were too scared to touch.

A few leaves were lying on the ground. That was all that remained of the tree.

I was no longer seven or eight years old.

I was thirteen.

Next year I would go to high school.

I no longer cried about everything.

But the burning pain in my chest was so bad it felt as if I was going to suffocate. I clenched my teeth and my fists.

It was stupid. I didn't know why I wanted to cry. It was just a stupid bloody tree. Thousands and thousands of them were chopped down every day and no one ever shed a tear about that.

'A tree should be for ever,' said a voice behind me.

I quickly wiped my eyes.

The caretaker appeared beside me but I didn't look at him.

'But nothing on this earth is for ever,' he continued in a soothing voice. 'What's most important is that you and Leila made sure the tree was really *seen*. In today's world that's more necessary than you think – to be noticed. Too many trees and animals and people have become invisible, or have simply disappeared, without anyone remembering them.' For a moment he put his hand on my shoulder. 'You and Leila are welcome to pop in for coffee any time.'

Then Uncle John turned around and walked back to the bowling green.

I let out a deep breath and stared at the sawn-off stump sticking out of the ground. I thought of Mr Fourie, who said I had a rich imagination, and I thought of what the caretaker had just said.

Maybe I could imagine that the tree had only become invisible…

I pictured a rough, thick trunk growing out of the sawn-off stump. The trunk grew taller and taller and taller. From the trunk sprouted thick, low branches, close to each other – the kind of branches that are perfect to teach a little girl how to climb a tree. The trunk reached higher into the sky, higher and higher and higher, until it made you dizzy to look at it. It split into smaller and smaller branches. The tree was exploding into leaves. Birds came to sit on the branches, chirping and twittering; the wind rustled the leaves; the rough bark was basking in the afternoon sun. And somewhere on the bark, in a secret place among the leaves, appeared a heart with two letters inside it.

I smiled.

Below the last composition in my exercise book Mr Fourie had written, *Keep writing such good compositions! I'm going to miss your talent next year.* I got ninety-five percent for that composition.

I hoped that the following year I would get a chance to write a composition about a tree that appeared out of the ground. It would be a good composition, I just knew it. The caretaker was right: it was great to be noticed – even if it was only because you wrote good compositions.

At that moment I thought I understood why Mrs Merriman dyed her hair pink, wore pink clothes and walked from house to house to collect money for the SPCA.

Why Joy shaved her head, had her nose pierced and became Killer.

Maybe I even understood why Mum spent so much time on her Very Important Court Case; why Dad wanted a bigger sign for his shop; why Adrian had been thinking up clever plans to make money since he was small.

It was to be noticed.

I smiled. It actually made sense.

OK, except maybe for Adrian. He was probably a born money-grabber.

It was no fun always being Marnus-in-the-middle. The one who wasn't a good swimmer, didn't have hordes of girlfriends and wasn't allergic to schoolwork. The one who couldn't read fluently at the age of five and wasn't constantly busy with all kinds of moneymaking plans.

I thought I had finally worked out what made me sit in the tree with Leila in the first place.

Most importantly, I thought I understood why Leila had started a petition to save the tree.

Sometimes you need to be noticed – even if it's by your own dad.

'Marnus!'

I swung around in surprise when the caretaker called my name. He had stopped some distance away from me and had turned around.

'Can I tell you a secret?'

I nodded.

'That first evening, your mum came to look for me at the bowling green. She offered me money to keep an eye on you and Leila all the time. I refused to take the money, but I promised her to take good care of you both. I could see she was terribly worried about you.'

I couldn't believe my ears. So that was why the caretaker would come every evening and sit under the tree with Leila and her mum and me. And that was why he brought us coffee and looked so angry when it seemed like things were getting out of control with the students.

I smiled.

My family was weird.

'Merry Christmas to you, Marnus!' said the caretaker. 'Oh yes, I almost forgot to tell you – Mrs Merriman sends her regards. She invited me to have lunch with her on Christmas Day.' He turned around and walked off.

The caretaker might be old but was it my imagination or had his eyes just sparkled the way Donovan's did when he spoke of Melissa?

'Merry Christmas, Uncle John!' I called.

19

Green Leaves

Number 9 Begonia Street wasn't far from the park. Fortunately Junior du Toit had asked Leila her surname for his newspaper article, otherwise I wouldn't have been able to look up their address in the phone directory the previous night.

The house looked almost as I'd imagined it would. It had a sunny porch covered in purple flowers. I was sure Leila would know the name of the plant with the purple flowers. The lawn was in need of mowing. In a sunny spot on the porch sat a ginger cat who looked at me through lazy, half-open eyes as I pressed the buzzer at the gate.

I waited for quite a while but no one opened the door.

Disappointed, I turned around, but then, out of the corner of my eye, I saw a curtain move.

'Leila!' I called.

At first I thought she was going to ignore me but then the front door opened.

Leila walked to the gate. She was wearing shorts and a light-green T-shirt, and she was barefoot. Her hair was tied up in a ponytail.

'Hello, Marnus,' she said.

I expected her to be angry but she sounded quite friendly. By then I had learned one thing, even though I hadn't known her for that long: with Leila you never knew exactly what to expect.

'How did you know where I live?'

I shrugged. 'I knew it was within walking distance of the park and I've read the odd spy story so I've picked up some tips.'

She smiled.

I cleared my throat. 'Erm...I guess you saw...I mean, the tree.'

She just nodded. That morning her eyes looked even bluer.

'I'm sorry,' I said.

Leila shook her head. 'It isn't your fault. Things got a bit...out of hand. You want to come inside? I'm busy packing but you can quickly come for a cool drink if you want. We don't have organic fruit juice but there's Coke in the fridge.' There was a slight reproach in her voice but I could hear that she was actually joking.

'That freaking Nature's Gift cold drink tasted like dishwashing water,' I muttered. 'So...erm... are you going on holiday?'

She nodded. 'My mum and I are going to spend Christmas with my seaside granny. And after that I'm going away with my dad for a few days,' she said as if it was the most normal thing on Earth. 'It's probably high time I got to know my stepmother and little stepbrother.'

I bent down and picked up the black plastic bag at my feet. 'Then I'm just in time,' I said. 'This is for you. Merry Christmas – even though it's still four days away.'

On the way there people had stared at me strangely. I guess they didn't often see someone walking three blocks carrying a tree with a red ribbon tied around its trunk. But what the heck – it wasn't exactly the strangest thing I had done in the past few days.

Leila unlocked the gate and took the small tree from me.

'A white karee,' she said.

'Scientific name: *Rhus pendulina*.' I pretended to be clever. 'I hope you have space in the garden. The man at the nursery said they grow very fast but you'll still have to wait a few years before it's big enough to climb into.'

'You're never too old to climb a tree,' said Leila with a smile. She caressed the leaves of the tree and looked at me, cocking her head. 'Marnus, do you remember what you asked me that first day when you opened the door with the dishcloth in your hand?'

Embarrassed, I cleared my throat. 'Erm...I asked whether you were there for kissing lessons.'

Unexpectedly, she leaned forward and kissed me.

It was just a quick kiss that merely brushed my lips but my heart started doing strange things in my chest.

The sun suddenly felt much warmer on my face and shoulders.

The wind gently ruffled my hair.

And a tingling sensation went through my arms and legs.

As if, at any moment, leaves and blossoms would sprout from my body.

Acknowledgements

A lot of people helped to make this book possible, and I owe them so many thanks.

First of all, a huge thank you (and many kisses) to Elize, Mia and Emma for your love, patience and encouragement all those times when I'm off climbing trees in my head.

My publisher, Miemie du Plessis at LAPA Publishers, has had my back since pretty much for ever. Thanks (and a super-duper-sized milkshake) for believing in my first story when I was only twenty-one, and sticking it out with me since.

Kobus Geldenhuys did the English translation, and Madeleine Stevens did the copy-editing – and I think they both did an amazing job. I really appreciate your hard work and gentle approach to the story.

I am extremely grateful to BookTrust and everyone involved in the In Other Words project. This groundbreaking initiative is making books spread their wings all over the world.

And finally, thank you to my editor, Shadi Doostdar, as well as Paul Nash, Kate Bland and the rest of the team at Oneworld and Rock the Boat, who put their faith in this book and made me feel right at home from the very start.